DEEP
WATER

BOOKS BY WATT KEY

Alabama Moon
Dirt Road Home
Fourmile
Terror at Bottle Creek
Hideout
Deep Water

DEEP WATER

WATT KEY

SQUARE
FISH

FARRAR STRAUS GIROUX · NEW YORK

An imprint of Macmillan Publishing Group, LLC
175 Fifth Avenue, New York, NY 10010
mackids.com

Square Fish and the Square Fish logo are trademarks of Macmillan and
are used by Farrar Straus Giroux under license from Macmillan.

Our books may be purchased in bulk for promotional, educational, or
business use. Please contact your local bookseller or the Macmillan Corporate
and Premium Sales Department at (800) 221-7945 ext. 5442 or by
email at MacmillanSpecialMarkets@macmillan.com.

Library of Congress Cataloging-in-Publication Data

Names: Key, Watt, author.
Title: Deep water / Watt Key.
Description: New York : Farrar Straus Giroux, 2018. | Summary: When a dive off
    the coast of Alabama goes horribly wrong, twelve-year-old Julie and one of her
    father's scuba clients struggle to survive after reaching an abandoned oil rig.
Identifiers: LCCN 2017023579 (print) | LCCN 2017038542 (ebook) |
    ISBN 978-1-250-29439-5 (paperback) | ISBN 978-0-374-30656-4 (ebook)
Subjects: | CYAC: Survival—Fiction. | Scuba diving—Fiction. | Oil well drilling
    rigs—Fiction. | Adventure and adventurers—Fiction. | Friendship—Fiction. |
    Family problems—Fiction. | Mexico, Gulf of—Fiction.
Classification: LCC PZ7.K516 (ebook) | LCC PZ7.K516 Dee 2018 (print) |
    DDC [Fic]—dc23
LC record available at https://lccn.loc.gov/2017023579

Originally published in the United States by Farrar Straus Giroux
First Square Fish edition, 2019
Square Fish logo designed by Filomena Tuosto

3   5   7   9   10   8   6   4

AR: 4.7 / LEXILE: 720L

Special thanks to Lewis Philips and Chas Broughton for their help with the technical aspects of this story. And thanks to the great crew at Gulf Coast Divers for some fun scuba diving.

REGULATOR

MASK

AIR TANK

BUOYANCY
COMPENSATOR
DEVICE "BCD"

GAUGE CONSOLE
(HOUSES COMPASS,
DEPTH GAUGE,
AND AIR GAUGE)

DIVE WATCH

WEIGHT BELT

SPEAR GUN

WETSUIT

DIVE KNIFE

BOOTIES

FINS

DEEP WATER

1

THE GPS BEEPED, SIGNALING OUR ARRIVAL AT THE DIVE SITE. DAD slowed our old twenty-nine-foot trawler, the *Barbie Doll*, and I sat up and peered through the windows of the wheelhouse. We'd lost sight of land over an hour ago. Nearly thirty miles off the coast of Gulf Shores, Alabama, there was nothing to see above the waterline except for an endless expanse of swells shimmering in the sunlight. But off our port side I saw a swarm of fish descending in a column through the jade-colored water.

"You're right," I said to him. "There's fish all over it."

Somewhere in the depths below were two army tanks, government surplus from the Vietnam War. Three years before, my dad, Gibson Sims, had been hired to tow them out on a barge and push them into the water, where they sank to the seafloor to create an artificial fish habitat. Then, through an unfortunate occurrence that had nothing to do with him, the coordinates were lost and the tanks presumably abandoned forever beneath over a hundred feet of water.

It wasn't until a week ago that Dad found the tanks again. He said they'd attracted barnacles and tiny fish, which in turn attracted larger fish until the tanks were a fully developed reef. Now the reef was home to hundreds of varieties of fish and resembled an amusement park for sea creatures.

I was eager to see the reef, but most important to me that day was knowing these tanks could save Dad's charter business. We needed to make sure our clients, Hank Jordan and his son, Shane, had a good dive and told others about it.

"Yep," Dad said under his breath, "they'll get their money's worth."

I sensed he was nervous, too. He knew as well as I did how important this dive was.

I looked at him. He was barefoot in his swim trunks and a faded madras plaid shirt. His wild gray hair seemed permanently stiff with dried salty water. His face was a little sunburned, but he was still fresh and youthful-looking, like a boy trapped in a middle-aged body. He was a big bear of a man, but he often reminded me of an overgrown kid. And despite the family and financial problems we'd left ashore, I felt proud of him for the first time in a long while.

Just the anticipation of a scuba dive can melt your worries away. And once you descend into the blue-green depths it seems the rest of the world doesn't even exist. I feel like an astronaut drifting in silent, immense space. Only this space is not dark and empty, but full of colorful sea life. Nothing compares to the thrill and peacefulness of hanging weightlessly in this mysterious world of exotic creatures.

Dad glanced behind us, making sure our clients were still seated on the back deck. The location of the tanks was a valuable secret, and he didn't trust them to keep their eyes off our navigation equipment. Those two were about as difficult as they came. Both Mr. Jordan and Shane spoke to us rudely, didn't listen to advice, and were always arguing with each other. Dad was still stewing over Mr. Jordan insulting his charter operation that morning and looking down on me like a twelve-year-old girl had no place on the boat. Normally he would have told them to take their business elsewhere, but today they were paying nearly four times our usual rate—and we needed the money.

"I don't think they can see the GPS from back there," I assured him.

Dad frowned doubtfully and wiped his forehead again with a hand towel.

"How do you feel?" I asked.

On the way out I'd noticed him sweating and wiping his face. I guessed it was his diabetes and got him a candy bar, but he didn't seem any better.

"Dad?" I said again.

He didn't like talking about his health and didn't seem concerned about it either. I felt like I was constantly having to monitor him. I recalled a dive the summer before when we'd had to surface early because his blood sugar was low and he got disoriented at fifty feet. It was episodes like that which worried me.

"Dad, are you able to go down or not?"

It was over a hundred feet to the seafloor, and I wasn't a certified dive master like he was. I'd certainly been that deep many times before, but it wouldn't look very professional to the Jordans if I replaced Dad as their guide. But if something were to happen to Dad at those depths, people like the Jordans couldn't be relied on to help him.

"Mr. Jordan won't like me guiding them," I said.

"I'm not worried about what that jerk likes and doesn't like," Dad replied. "Those two are reckless enough to get

6

themselves in trouble down there. And I don't want you mixed up in it."

"I can handle myself," I said.

"I know . . . But I can still be worried about it."

Dad's the toughest person I know. I once saw him stitch a cut on his leg with a fishhook and fishing line so he wouldn't have to end a dive trip early. I knew if he decided to send me in his place he would have to be feeling really bad. But one of the most important rules of diving is if you don't feel right, don't go down. There are already too many things that can go wrong with a person's body in the depths without adding other complications.

I exited the wheelhouse to find the Jordans arguing about their spearguns and who got to take the larger one. Shane was about my age. He and I had been in the same class at elementary school when I lived with my parents in Gulf Shores. That was before Mom and Dad divorced and I moved to Atlanta with Mom, leaving Dad behind in our old house. Now Shane was taller than I remembered, and he'd grown his hair out so that it hung almost to his shoulders in a style popular with local surfers. He wore a Salt Life T-shirt, AFTCO shorts, and deck sandals, all of it looking like he'd pulled the price tags off that morning. He's smart, athletic, wealthy, and good-looking if you like the type. I don't like the type.

Even when we were younger, he struck me as one of

those kids who complain about everything like they're in a constant battle with an unfair world when I can't imagine they know anything about unfair.

Shane's father was a local attorney, but his face was on interstate billboards clear to Montgomery. On the advertisements Hank Jordan looked tall and young in a trim, expensive pinstripe suit. He held a stern expression and had his arms crossed over his chest like he'd just solved a big problem. What I saw standing before me in a fishing shirt, shorts, and Crocs was a shorter, wrinkled version of the man on the signs. He looked a lot more like an aging weasel.

"This it?" Mr. Jordan asked.

"Yes," I replied as I made my way up to the bow. "We're at the Malzon tanks."

That's what Dad and I called them, after the guy who hired us to put them in the water.

I unfastened the anchor chain and held it while Dad maneuvered the *Barbie Doll*, taking it in and out of gear and assessing the current. Finally I heard him tap on the window glass. I let the chain slip from my hands and heard the anchor plunge into the water. For scuba divers this basic piece of boating equipment is much more than something to keep us moored in place—it's our guide to the seafloor and our lifeline back to the boat. I leaned over the railing and watched the white rope stream into the depths. The visibility was decent, but the current was strong up top. I hoped it wasn't as swift down below. That's one problem with scuba diving. You don't really know what dangers you're up against until you're deep into them.

2

I WAITED UNTIL THE ROPE GREW TAUT AND I HEARD THE ENGINE groan as Dad backed against it. Then I could see by the way the rope stretched and dripped water that the anchor was holding. I looked at Dad and gave him the okay signal with my fingers. He shut off the engine and I threw out the safety line, a smaller rope that floated alongside and that we used to get ourselves to and from the anchor rope once we were in the water. When I returned to the stern I found the Jordans arguing again. This time Shane was complaining that Mr. Jordan had left his dive gloves at the house. It seemed there was no end to the things they could find to fuss over.

Just then Dad stepped out of the wheelhouse and stood watching them. "As soon as you guys work out your problems I can get you in the water."

Shane frowned, shook his head with disgust, and gave his dive bag a kick. "Jackass," he mumbled to his father.

Mr. Jordan ignored his son. He zipped up his wetsuit and grabbed his buoyancy compensator device, or BCD. This is an inflatable vest used to counter a diver's weight belt and control how fast we ascend and descend. After the breathing apparatus, called the regulator, it's the most important piece of equipment a diver wears.

"The anchor should be close to the north tank," Dad continued. "But there's fish all over both of them, and you shouldn't have any problems finding your way around."

I studied Dad, still wondering if he was going or not.

Mr. Jordan carried his gear to the air tanks strapped to the gunnels. He pulled one of the tanks and began clipping it to his BCD. Shane was in his wetsuit already. He grabbed his own BCD and carried it over toward the tanks.

"Go ahead and suit up, Julie," Dad said.

Mr. Jordan looked at him.

"She's going to take you down today," Dad said.

"You've got to be kidding me," Shane said.

"Gib, I'm not paying all this money for some kid to guide me," Mr. Jordan said.

"You don't need a guide. She's only going to watch for your own safety. She's made more dives than the two of you combined, so you're in good hands."

"What's *your* problem?" Mr. Jordan asked.

"I'm not feeling well."

"You might have told us that before now."

"Well, Hank, you want me to pull anchor and start back in?"

Mr. Jordan studied him and I saw a look of intense dislike pass between them. "We came this far," he finally said. "We're going down there."

"That's what I figured," Dad said, turning back to the wheelhouse. "Finish getting into your gear and roll off."

Dad went back inside, and I got my wetsuit and booties out of a plastic storage bin. I was already wearing shorts and a tank top pulled over a white skinsuit, a thin layer that protects against jellyfish and makes it easier to pull on the neoprene. I removed my shorts and tank top and pulled the wetsuit on. Then I clipped my weight belt around my waist, and strapped my dive knife to my ankle. As I fastened my BCD to one of the remaining tanks I kept an eye on the Jordans. All of the gear they pulled from their bags was new and top-of-the-line. Among these items were pony tanks, small air tanks about the size of fire extinguishers. They each strapped one to their BCDs next to their main tank. This was as much as saying they planned on staying down longer than they should, and Dad wasn't going to like that.

Shane strapped his knife to his ankle and grabbed his speargun. "We better shoot something," he said to his dad like I wasn't there.

"I doubt he's ever made this much money off one trip in his life," Mr. Jordan muttered. "You'd think he'd show a little more effort to accommodate us."

"He'd go down if he could," I said.

They ignored me.

"Well," Shane said, "at least she can help us carry the fish up. I don't know why else we even need her."

"My name is Julie," I snapped. "And if you want me to stay behind, I'm sure Dad won't have a problem with that."

Dad stepped onto the back deck again. I saw him eye the Jordans' pony tanks. He frowned and knelt beside my BCD, checked that my air valve was on, and clicked the purge on my regulator a few times to make sure air was flowing through it. Once he was satisfied, he hefted the gear onto the railing. Together, the tank, BCD, and regulator weigh nearly forty pounds. My weight belt was already ten pounds. All of this combined is too much for me to wear out of the water, so Dad usually lowers it over the side for me.

Dad motioned with his chin for me to get in. I put my

mask around my neck, spit in it, and rubbed the spit around with my finger. It's a trick to keep the glass from fogging and works almost as well as the more expensive defog drops the Jordans were using. Then I slipped the mask over my face, pulled on my dive fins, and rolled overboard. The current swept me alongside the hull until I was able to grab the safety line. A moment later the Jordans splashed in next to me and bobbed to the surface with their spearguns held over their heads.

"Check them out," Dad said from above as they grabbed on to the safety line.

I swam around behind each of them, checking that the valves were all the way open on their tanks.

"Everybody check your air meter and give me a thumbs-up if it shows full," Dad said.

Each of them had a console about the size of a telephone handset connected to their tank with another hose. The console contains an air gauge, a compass, and a depth meter. Dad and I still preferred the older analog gauges, while the Jordans were using the newer digital models. They inspected their air readings and signaled okay.

"Take two breaths out of your regulators and give me another thumbs-up," Dad said.

Their regulators checked out.

"I want to remind you that this dive is a hundred and five feet. I recommend you stay on the bottom no longer than twenty minutes. Julie, when you start up, stop at twenty feet. Make sure you have enough air to hang there for fifteen minutes."

"We've got ponies," Mr. Jordan said.

"I see that. And you can do what you want. You signed waivers. But I'm telling you what I recommend."

"We know what we're doing," Mr. Jordan said.

"The current up top is pretty strong today," Dad continued. "Hopefully it won't be bad on the floor. When you get back to the boat, hold on to the safety line and I'll help all of you get your equipment in."

Dad lowered my BCD, tank, and hoses to me. He held the top of the tank while I worked my arms into the BCD and buckled the waist strap. I took a couple of test breaths from my regulator, checked my gauges, and gave Dad a thumbs-up signal. Then he leaned close and said, "Twenty minutes' bottom time, Julie. No matter what's going on. Understand?"

I nodded. He gave me a long look that told me he didn't like the situation any more than I did. Our clients were an accident waiting to happen, but I was about to find an even bigger problem waiting in the depths below.

3

THERE IS NOTHING MORE FUN THAN SCUBA DIVING. BUT LIKE ANY other extreme sport, it can also be dangerous. Most people think it's all about how much stored air you have, but it's mostly about depth and time. After you descend below thirty feet the water pressure begins to force nitrogen from the air you breathe into your bloodstream and lungs. The deeper you go, and the longer you stay at those depths, the faster you absorb those dangerous gas bubbles. You can stay on the seafloor only a certain amount of time before you have to return; you rise to the surface slowly and make safety stops at the shallower depths to let the bubbles leak back out of your blood. If you ignore the time limits and stops or do them wrong, and you come up too quickly, you face your worst nightmare: the bends. If you get bent, you can become paralyzed when you reach the surface.

Dad once described the bends to me with a bottle of Sprite. He explained that the carbonation in the soft drink is made by filling the bottle with compressed gas and then sealing it under pressure. Then he shook up the plastic bottle and set it in front of me.

"That's how much pressure your body's under during a scuba dive. What happens if you take the top off that thing?"

"It'll spew everywhere."

"That's right," he said.

Dad grabbed the Sprite and barely twisted the cap so that I heard a slight hiss of escaping pressure.

"So you let the gas out slowly," he said.

I watched the gas bubbles gradually rising to the top of the soda, and I suddenly understood.

Every diver's body has a different tolerance for the depths, but we all use charts and computers that calculate the recommended time limits and duration of the safety stops. That's how Dad came up with twenty minutes on the bottom and a fifteen-minute stop on the way up. If you decide to stay down longer than what the calculations advise, it gets more complicated. These dives are referred to as decompression, or "deco," dives. Additional safety stops are needed and we have to make sure we have enough air left to wait them out. The risk of getting bent is much higher. Apparently the Jordans were willing to take this risk.

By the time I was clipped into my BCD and breathing through my regulator, our clients were already at the anchor rope and heading down. I looked up at Dad one last time.

"Make sure they get to the tanks," he said. "Then back off."

I nodded to him again, flipped my fins, and gave chase.

I swam down with one hand sliding along the anchor rope. I was soon in the midst of yellow and red and blue and green fish of all sizes, darting about like parade confetti. Then I saw the Jordans, already thirty feet below, descending the edge of the fish column in a cloud of bubbles. Divers should always stay together, but they were clearly not concerned about me. And the current felt dangerously swift. Dad might have called off the dive if he'd actually felt it. But the Jordans weren't about to turn around, and it was my responsibility to watch them until my twenty minutes were up and do what I could in the case of an emergency.

Even after hundreds of dives I still get nervous when I can no longer see the surface or what's below me. I also get nervous as the sunlight is filtered away and the water grows colder. That's when you know you've entered the danger zone: another world, an aquatic wilderness where humans are not meant to be.

Despite my fears, I knew the feeling was a lot like the sensation I get inching up the first big hill of a roller coaster. It's scary, but I've done it before and I know I'm safe. And the reward beyond makes it all worthwhile.

As the water pressure built against my eardrums I stopped, pinched my nose, and blew against the inside of my ears until I heard them squeak and clear with escaping air. I had to do this about every five feet to keep my eardrums from bursting.

Another fifty feet down I saw a dark blur that I assumed was the north tank. The Jordans were moving along the seafloor now, slowly working against the current, heading for the south tank, where, mysteriously, the fish column seemed more concentrated.

I descended ten more feet and paused again to relieve the pressure on my ears. The tank was clearly visible now, a strange, ghostly relic of war that was both enticing and fearsome. The giant steel body, the gun barrel, and even the tracks were still intact, like the tank had driven into the water and parked there on the endless plain of rippled sand. I finally felt oriented and safe and allowed the thrill of the adventure to sweep over me. I thought about all the tourists in Gulf Shores, their cars loaded with skim boards, float toys, foldout chairs, coolers, and sun umbrellas. They parked alongside the highway and lugged their equipment out onto the beach. They splashed at its edges and stared out across the vast expanse of it, but that was as much of the water as they'd get. Most of them never even dreamed of going to the places we went, miles out beyond the curve of the horizon, into the mysterious depths of a silent, colorful world.

But my excitement was short-lived. Fear crept over me again as I dropped closer to the tank and saw the anchor. It was resting behind the gun barrel on top of the hatch cover, an unlikely drop. When I reached it I noted that it was barely clinging to a thin lip of steel. I could see it shifting and hear the points of the flukes scratching against the metal. The strange noise explained why the fish had fled to the other tank. But I wasn't concerned about the fish. If any pressure was taken off the rope, the anchor could fall out of place. And with the boat straining against it, the dangers of resetting it were too great to risk. The heavy steel hardware could spring back and stab me with its sharp flukes or knock me unconscious.

Had the Jordans been with me, I would have signaled an immediate ascent. If the anchor pulled, Dad would be adrift, trailing our lifeline with him. He wouldn't have time to make another drop before we needed to surface. Certainly not by himself. And without the anchor rope to guide us up, we'd be swept away with the current.

I contemplated resurfacing without the Jordans, but that option seemed no better. Even if Dad and I could reset the anchor in time for their ascent, we'd never be able to drop it in the same place and it was likely they'd never find it.

There was no easy answer. All I could do was try to keep an eye on this new problem and the Jordans at the same time.

4

I PULLED MYSELF DOWN TO THE LEE SIDE OF THE TANK TO GET out of the current. Then I knelt on the seafloor, grabbed my gauge console, and got a reading from the compass. Once I got my bearings I withdrew my knife, held it before me, and kicked toward the other tank. The current was coming at me sideways, so I had to keep my stomach low and stab the knife into the sand to keep from getting swept away. In this manner I managed to locate the south tank after a few minutes. It was clouded with snapper, grouper, triggerfish, and smaller reef fish of all sizes and colors. There could be no question that the Jordans were getting what they paid for.

I saw what looked like Mr. Jordan about thirty feet away, taking a lane snapper off his spear and running his fish stringer through its gills. I didn't see Shane. I was anxious to get back to the north tank and keep an eye on the anchor. I searched the blue haze around me again and thought I saw a trace of bubbles off to my left. I started that way and it wasn't long before I saw Shane chasing an amberjack. I stopped and tapped my tank with the butt of my knife, but he didn't look at me. I checked my watch and gauge console again. I'd been down nine minutes and I had two-thirds of my air left.

Plenty of time, I told myself.

I watched Shane shoot and miss. The gun resembled a crossbow, except in place of the bow were three rubber bands as thick as my thumb. These bands propelled a four-foot steel spear that was attached to a fifteen-foot-long cable. Shane retrieved the spear and reseated it on the gun. As he struggled to re-cock the rubber bands I made my way over to him. I tapped him on the shoulder and he looked at me. I pointed down at my watch and signaled seven minutes with my fingers. He ignored me and turned his attention back to the speargun. I didn't know what else to do, so I decided it was best to return and keep an eye on the anchor.

I could no longer see the north tank from where I was, so I studied my compass and tried to work backward to get an accurate heading. I knew I'd gone south and then angled off to my left, which would have been east. So I determined I needed a northwest heading for my return. But as soon as I started in that direction I realized I'd underestimated the current and I was almost swimming directly against it this time. I kicked furiously and stabbed my knife into the sand to pull myself along, but it was nearly impossible and I felt myself breathing heavily and using up air at an alarming rate. I stabbed and kicked, stabbed and kicked, until finally I had to stop and rest.

I looked at my watch. Sixteen minutes. I had four minutes to get back to the anchor and start up.

Not going to make it.

I began to play out scenarios in my head, visualizing what it would be like if I had to surface without the anchor rope. I could be swept a mile away while I was making my safety stop. If I could even control my safety stop. It was hard to maintain a certain depth without something to hold on to, especially in such a strong current. At the moment I needed to calm down and try to make it to the anchor.

Despite all my years of scuba diving, this was the first real emergency I'd ever faced. But it was situations like this Dad had trained me for. And I suddenly found my life depending on everything he'd taught me.

The number-one rule in a diving emergency: *Don't*

panic. The more you panic, the more air you breathe and the more bad decisions you make.

I told myself to calm down and focus on reaching the anchor.

I began moving my legs steadily against the current and plunging my knife into the sand in a methodical way. One foot at a time I made progress, my eyes trained on where I thought the tank should be. And slowly it came into focus. Once I saw it I got a burst of energy and kicked with everything I had. I knew I'd be outside of twenty minutes, but as long as I had the anchor rope to hold on to I could control additional stops.

My mind raced as I tried to recall exactly how long we'd made our safety stops on a deco dive last summer. But then I was distracted by something else. When I was about twenty feet away I realized all my fears about the dive that day were coming true. The anchor was gone.

For a moment I was in disbelief. I thought maybe I'd circled back to the wrong tank. I jabbed my knife into the sand and grabbed my gauge console. It showed I was still heading in the right direction. Then I looked up again and studied the seafloor down-current of me. I saw faint drag marks in the sand telling me for certain that the anchor had sprung loose.

I glanced at my watch. Thirty minutes had passed. My body was surely saturated with nitrogen gas.

I checked my air gauge, and my heart skipped a beat when I saw that three-fourths of my air was gone. I had to start my ascent immediately. And I had to try not to panic.

I looked for the Jordans, but they were nowhere in sight.

Get out of here, I thought.

I pressed my inflator button to inject air into my BCD and felt myself begin to rise slowly off the seafloor. I saw the sand ripples race beneath me as the current took hold and swept me along. I held the gauge console before my face. Ninety feet. Eighty feet. The sand ripples soon blurred into a blank, flat plain of yellowish-brown. I tried not to think about how far I was being swept from the dive site. I kept reminding myself to breathe slowly and maintain a controlled ascent.

As I neared forty feet I decided to make my first safety stop. I let air out of my BCD until I was having to kick to keep from sinking. It was only then that I realized how tired my legs were. But to be certain that all the nitrogen was out of my bloodstream, I knew I had to stay there for at least ten minutes. I checked my air gauge. I was alarmed to see only one-eighth supply remaining.

I put a little more air back into my BCD so I didn't have to kick so much, keeping my eyes on the depth gauge. For what seemed like an eternity I hovered there. Trapped in a dead zone of liquid space, being swept helplessly farther and farther away. My compass showed I was moving to the southeast. I didn't want to look at my air gauge again. It would only worry me and make me breathe faster.

When my watch finally showed that I'd stayed ten minutes I kicked up to twenty feet and stopped again. At the shallower depths I'd use my air at a slower rate, but I knew I didn't have enough to last the twenty minutes I needed. I only hoped the deco stop at forty had been enough.

After eight minutes I felt my air running out. It feels like trying to breathe through a straw. I waited another two minutes until I was practically holding my breath, then I kicked for the surface. I was suddenly transported from a world of clicks and bubbles and hissing air into a world of sunlight and crisp sound.

The first thing that flashed through my mind was that none of my joints hurt. I felt fine. If I had the bends, it was only a mild case or it hadn't yet set in.

Then I looked around. The Gulf was rougher than I remembered. I kicked to peer above the waves and saw nothing but blue water clear to the horizon in every direction. I'd never dropped a weight belt before, but knew that once I was on the surface it was the first thing to go in an emergency. I had to get as buoyant as possible.

I unclipped the belt and let it sink into the depths. Then I fully inflated my BCD by blowing into the manual inflator mouthpiece. Finally there was nothing to do but float there and wonder what had happened to our boat and the Jordans and how long it would take before someone found me.

5

RISING AND FALLING WITH THE SWELLS, I TOLD MYSELF TO STAY calm.

Dad will come for me.

I let that thought sit in my head for a few seconds, trying to smother a darker truth.

If the anchor had pulled, as soon as he noticed Dad would have known to let the boat drift. He and I would have traveled at the same speed. And the boat would at least be within sight.

Then I thought that maybe it was too rough and I couldn't see far enough.

Maybe he's getting the Jordans out of the water. They

stayed down longer than me, so they won't have drifted as far.

But over it all, I thought about the Malzon tanks. Suddenly the word *Malzon* sounded sinister and brought forth a flood of painful memories. It seemed like everything started with those tanks. They were cursed.

When I was nine years old Dr. Malzon asked Dad to create a private fishing reef for him. Sometimes when his scuba charter business slowed in the winter Dad took unusual jobs like this to make ends meet. So he agreed and spent three days figuring out how to get the two tanks and an excavator loaded onto a borrowed barge. Then he woke me at three o'clock in the morning to help him make the drop.

We used the *Barbie Doll* to pull the barge out of the pass and into the smooth, inky-dark swells of the Gulf. Dad always added a little more adventure to a situation than some people (like my mom) thought was necessary, but that morning he insisted we needed to complete our mission under the cover of darkness. When building private reefs it's important that no one sees the drop and steals the coordinates.

Thirty miles out, Dad told me to take over the controls.

He instructed me to keep the *Barbie Doll* dead slow ahead into the wind while he went back onto the barge. As soon as I saw him drop the first tank I was to stop the engines, count to ten, and write down our GPS coordinates. I'd been driving the *Barbie Doll* since I was six, so his request was nothing unusual to me. And I've always been very particular about things, so he trusted me to write the numbers down accurately.

Dad pushed the first tank off the barge with the excavator and it made a tremendous splash that rocked the boat. I shut down the engines as he shoved the second one overboard. Then I counted as we drifted past and they sank to their permanent resting place. I was writing the coordinates from the GPS on a Post-it note when he came back into the wheelhouse. He didn't even look at my numbers. Someone had paid for them and their secrecy, and Dad is always a man of his word to the extreme.

Not two weeks after Dad delivered the coordinates for the tanks, Dr. Malzon died of a brain aneurysm. He hadn't paid for the work yet, and Dad didn't feel it was appropriate to approach Mrs. Malzon about it. As Dad saw it, the tanks now belonged to us.

Mom was angry when he told her he wasn't even going to ask to be paid for four days of his time and expenses. I heard them arguing about it late into the night. I'd heard Mom express her frustrations with him before, but it was usually over little things like something he forgot or something he was late for. And then I'd catch her smiling at him later like none of the fussing meant much. But this time it was different. This time she sounded like she was going to stay mad.

Somehow Dad got his way with the tanks that night. And I remember the excitement in his eyes as he came into my room, sat on my bedside, and told me of his dream. Like the argument with Mom hadn't even happened.

"In a year there's going to be fish all over those things," he said. "People are going to pay big money to dive them . . . as soon as I find them again."

Dad spent the rest of the winter trying to relocate the tanks. He had a chart taped beside the steering wheel lined with a search grid that encompassed five square miles. He motored slowly along the gridlines, studying the bottom plotter for anomalies. The plotter bounced sound waves off the seafloor, and he needed to be directly over a target for it to register on the electronic graph. There is relatively little structure in that part of the Gulf. If you were to drain the water, the seafloor would look like a vast desert, dotted with the occasional artificial reef. If you don't have exact coordinates for something, you ordinarily won't find it. On a good day Dad would locate one or two items of interest. Then he'd make note of their GPS coordinates so that he could dive them later.

Even when I hadn't yet learned to dive, I went out with him on the weekends and stayed on the boat while he suited up in his scuba gear and descended the anchor rope to investigate items of interest from the week before. If there was any kind of emergency I could always radio for help and even drive the boat. Occasionally he found another artificial reef consisting of a rusty car body or boat hull. Most of the time it was an old ghost town of rubble, long since eroded and fished out. Sometimes it was nothing but a bucket. None of it was as large and impressive as the Malzon tanks.

When the diving business picked up again in the spring, Dad and I continued to look for the tanks when he didn't have a paid trip. In spite of Mom's reluctance, he taught me how to scuba dive that summer. I made hundreds of dives with him. I was a natural, he said. A regular sea otter. And by the time school started again he figured I'd made more dives than any other nine-year-old in the world. And I could tell he was proud of that thought.

As Dad continued with his obsession over the tanks I began to notice him and Mom arguing more, although I didn't know what it was about. Then, right before

Christmas, Dad told me he was giving up on the search.

"It's not meant to be," he said. "Besides, it's only a couple of tanks."

The following summer he focused more on his clients' trips again. I didn't know it, but Mom had already applied for a position with a law firm in Atlanta. And she'd already given Dad the divorce papers. As part of the divorce deal I would go live with her and spend summers with Dad.

He acted like nothing was happening. Like it was something that he could fix, only he hadn't quite figured out how. I don't think he truly believed it was all real until the day near the end of August when Mom and I drove away, pulling a U-Haul trailer packed with our things.

"I have dreams, too," Mom said to me. "And sometimes it's hard for two people with different dreams to be married."

I'd never thought about parents chasing dreams. Maybe because it seemed like Dad was already living his, owning his own dive shop and guiding scuba charters. And Mom seemed content practicing at a local law firm that specialized in insurance work. Now suddenly she revealed she'd always wanted to be a successful corporate attorney and Gulf Shores didn't have the opportunities for that. But I had a feeling there was more to it.

"How come you never talked about it before?" I asked her on the drive north.

"Just because I didn't talk about it doesn't mean I wasn't thinking it," she replied stubbornly.

I was confused and angry. I wanted to take Dad's side, but I didn't understand how he could let this happen. He was always able to fix anything. And he must not have cared enough about our family to repair it.

"How can you be married for twelve years and then want a divorce?" I said to her.

"People change, Julie," she replied.

I sensed she was referring to Dad's obsession with the Malzon tanks, but he'd always been excited about one thing or another. Even before the tanks. I'd never known a person to get so excited about waking up in the morning. Every day to him was an obsession in itself.

I stayed angry with Mom that whole school year. I wanted to go home and be with Dad. But last summer, when I finally did return to Gulf Shores, I didn't find the father I'd left behind. He'd lost a lot of weight, and his solid, good-natured grin had been replaced with a nervous, twitchy smile. Our old house and his office were a mess. He was constantly forgetting things and drifting off in thought. And I felt like he was hiding things from me, things he didn't want Mom to know about.

With my help he managed to build up his paid trips

again, but he didn't seem to enjoy himself as much anymore. And sometimes, on the way back in from one of
our charters, I noticed him driving the *Barbie Doll* very
slowly, staring at the bottom plotter. I secretly suspected
he hadn't given up his search for the tanks.

I was right.

6

THE SUCTION OF MY MASK WAS STARTING TO BOTHER ME. I
pulled it off and put it below my chin and rubbed at my
face. Other than the rolling of the waves, everything was
quiet. There wasn't a bird overhead or a fish jumping.
Everything alive was below the water, somewhere beneath my dangling feet. And it was only a matter of time
before those living things began to investigate this strange
impostor dangling from their roof. Some of them I didn't
want to meet, especially sharks.

    I pushed the thought of predators from my mind and
began to reason out my situation. I was certain the Jordans had stayed down longer than me. If they used their

pony tanks they might have had another fifteen minutes of bottom time before they started their ascent and made deco stops. Once they left the seafloor they would have started drifting, so I didn't need to account for their hang time. When they surfaced, if they had not done so already, they would be about fifteen minutes up-current of me.

Regardless, they were going to be mad, and probably want their money back. Money Dad didn't have after buying fuel for our trip out.

Was it simply bad luck? How could things have gone so wrong? The Malzon tanks were supposed to fix everything.

It hadn't even been a week since Dad called to announce his big discovery. I had been resting on our living room sofa in Atlanta, studying for final exams. Mom was sitting beside me with her netbook in her lap, a legal pad on the cushion beside her, and a pen dangling from her mouth. If I'd known he was going to call, I would have picked up in my room where she couldn't hear. I didn't like being in the middle of things with them.

When the phone rang I grabbed the handset off the end table. Both of us already knew who it was without looking at the caller ID. Dad was the only person who rang the house phone anymore. I'd given him my cell phone number at least five times, but he'd likely lost it, if he'd even written it down. He's very particular and me-thodical when it involves things like the boat and his dive equipment, but scatterbrained when it comes to keeping the rest of his life organized.

"Hey, Dad," I said quietly.

I detected Mom shift uncomfortably beside me.

"I found them, Julie!" he exclaimed.

"Found what?"

"The tanks! The Malzon tanks!"

"When?"

"Today! I just got in. You think I'd wait to call you?"

Mom reached out for the handset. "Give me the phone, Julie," she said.

"Dad, Mom wants to talk to you," I said.

Dad hesitated. "Did she hear all that?" he asked.

"Hold on," I said.

Mom took the handset from me and put it to her ear. "Gib, she's going to be there in less than a week, okay? Can you hold off on the drama until then?"

Mom looked at the wall and rolled her eyes as she listened.

"Gib," she said. "Gib, that's enough . . . Listen to me. That's all great. I'm happy for you. Meanwhile, Julie's got exams and I'm overloaded with work."

Mom listened again. I heard Dad's muffled defense through the handset.

"Gib," she interrupted, "she'll be there in a few days. Okay? We're driving down this weekend."

Mom held the phone out to me again and I took it back from her.

"I'll be there on Saturday, Dad. We can talk about it then."

Dad sighed. "Yeah, okay. I got excited, you know. I wanted to tell you. I thought you'd be excited, too."

I desperately wished he could know what I felt over the telephone line.

"I am," I said. "It's just not a good time. *Okay?*"

Dad was silent.

"I'll see you on Saturday," I said.

"Okay, sweetheart. I'm looking forward to it."

"Me too, Dad. I love you. And I can't wait to see you."

I hung up the phone and turned to Mom. "You didn't have to be so snippy with him," I said.

Mom set her pen down and studied me. "Julie, do you really want to do this? Spend your entire summer down there?"

I couldn't believe she was asking me that. "It's the only time I get to see him, Mom."

"But you could go to basketball camp. You could spend time with your friends here."

"I have friends in Alabama, too."

Mom picked up her pen again and studied the legal pad. "Well, you live in Atlanta now," she said. "You'd be wise to invest more in your friends who live nearby."

I didn't understand. I was doing fine in Atlanta. I made straight A's in school. I was the point guard on the sixth-grade girls' basketball team and captain of the math team. I had plenty of friends. And she knew how much I missed home and loved being on the water with Dad.

"But I thought it was part of the deal," I said.

Mom looked at me again. "Yes," she said. "I suppose it's part of the deal. But it doesn't mean that I have to like it."

It was you who wanted to move, I thought. *It was you who came up with the deal in the first place.*

"I think he misses me, Mom," I said.

Mom sighed. "Of course he misses you, Julie. And it's not that I don't want you to see him. I only worry that you could be doing so much more with your summer than running a dive shop with your father."

"He needs my help."

Mom frowned. "He's a grown man. He should be able to take care of himself."

Mom spent a lot of time talking about how Dad needed to get his life together, but she didn't seem to be doing so well herself. She's a good attorney, maybe too good. Ever

41

since she joined the Reese and Attenborough law firm her caseload has been never-ending. Even the few moments we have together she's usually preoccupied. When she takes me to school in the mornings she's on her cell phone most of the drive. She doesn't get home until after seven o'clock, and even then she parks herself on the living room sofa and continues working. She even works most weekends, taking a little time off to make my basketball games. I can't remember her ever missing one of my games, but I do remember that most of the time she's sitting alone in the stands with her cell phone in her lap, tapping out texts and emails. The few times she's taken off for us to go to the mountains I can tell she's still thinking about work. Always thinking about work. Like it's the only thing in the world that really matters.

"I'm doing this for your future," she told me once.

If our future was all about having money, Mom had certainly solved that problem. Within a year of moving to Atlanta, we'd bought a house in Buckhead, one of the nicest neighborhoods in the city. Mom traded in her old Subaru for a new top-of-the-line Range Rover. We seemed to have everything money can buy.

But things were still terribly wrong.

On the outside Mom appears healthy. She runs five miles every morning, saying it clears her mind. She's thin and pretty with a great smile. But I rarely see her smile anymore. And every morning when I hear the rattle of her pill bottle, her anxiety medication, I wonder how healthy she is on the inside.

I didn't want any of what we had in Atlanta.

I just wanted us all together again.

7

I LOOKED AT MY WATCH. I'D BEEN BACK-KICKING AGAINST THE current for almost ten minutes and my legs were starting to tire again. I stopped and let the current resume taking me wherever it was I was going. It wasn't long before I thought I heard someone shout.

I spun and faced up-current and kicked myself above the waves. I didn't see anyone. I settled again and listened. Then I was certain that I heard something.

"Dad!"

I recognized Shane's voice. I started back-kicking again, certain that he wasn't far up-current of me. After a few minutes I peered above the waves and saw him drifting and staring away from me.

"Shane!" I called out.

He turned and looked at me. I saw he also had his mask hanging around his neck and his eyes were wide with fright.

"What happened?" he yelled at me.

I closed the distance between us and grabbed on to his BCD. He was trembling.

"The anchor pulled," I said. "Have you seen your dad?"

"No! I haven't seen him since we left the bottom! How did the anchor pull?"

I noticed his BCD wasn't full of air, so I grabbed his manual inflator and began blowing into it.

"I don't think his pony tank was working," Shane continued. "How did the anchor pull?"

You saw the anchor, too, I thought. *And both of you ignored it.*

I blew as much air into his BCD as it would take, then checked the straps on it to make sure they were tight.

"Have you dropped your weight belt?" I asked him.

Shane studied me like he didn't understand. I reached down to his waist and felt for the buckle to his belt. I didn't feel it, then remembered the Jordans had pocket weights. I brushed my hands over the sides of his BCD until I felt the bulge of the lead modules. I tore open the Velcro flaps and began pulling the weights out and dropping them.

Shane kicked and tried to get away from me. "What are you doing?"

I grabbed his arm and jerked him close again. "You need to get rid of them. Get as buoyant as you can."

He stopped resisting and let me pull the remaining modules.

"Where's the boat?" he said.

I shoved away from him and kicked and looked up-current above the waves. I didn't see anything and tried again, looking to my left. Then I saw Mr. Jordan floating not fifty yards from us.

"I see your dad!" I shouted. I turned on my back and started kicking toward him. "He's not far!"

Shane followed me as we approached his father through the rolling swells. As I drew closer I kept looking over my shoulder, wondering why Mr. Jordan wasn't saying anything. When I reached him I got my answer. Watery blood ran down from the base of his mask.

"Mr. Jordan," I said.

He turned his head, looked at me, and hacked out a raspy, gurgling cough.

I grabbed his mask and pulled it away from his face and blood spilled out of it into the water. His eyes blinked and stared back at me in a stunned way. I lowered the mask around his neck and began to pull his weights.

"What are you doing?" he said.

"Dropping your weight."

He coughed again and brushed my hand away. "Don't touch me," he said.

I started to argue, then I got a jolt of horror when I saw his fish stringer dragging with two snappers still attached at the end. About that time Shane arrived behind me.

"Dad!" he shouted.

"He's bent," I said.

"We're s-s-screwed," Shane stammered. "We're so screwed. Where is the boat?"

Suddenly I couldn't take any more of his yelling while I was trying to think. I spun around and punched him in the face with all my fear and anger. Shane coughed and sputtered and stared at me in disbelief.

"The boat's not here!" I said. "So we're going to do what we can. Go cut his fish stringer off while I try to stop his nose from bleeding."

Shane continued to stare at me.

"Now!" I shouted. "Sharks can smell those fish."

Shane finally nodded that he understood and swam behind his dad to cut the stringer.

"I've got to stop your nose from bleeding, Mr. Jordan," I said.

He didn't answer me.

"Okay?" I said.

"Don't touch my weights," he said.

"I won't. I need to tend to your nose."

Mr. Jordan coughed again and nodded. I pulled my knife from my ankle and sliced off a piece of the pocket flap of my BCD. I cut the material into two more pieces and balled them up and stuffed them into his nose.

"What happened, Dad?" Shane said.

"Pony tank didn't work," he mumbled. "I had to bail."

"My dad should be here soon," I said. "He's probably somewhere close."

Mr. Jordan coughed again and a bit of blood appeared at the edge of his mouth. I started to wipe it off, then thought it was better to leave it on his face than trail more scent in the water.

"I've got to get to a hospital," he mumbled.

"I know," I said.

Shane pulled himself close and studied his dad's face. Mr. Jordan cocked his eyes at him.

"I can't feel my arms and legs, son," he said.

I looked down at Mr. Jordan's hands and saw he'd dropped his speargun at some point.

"I stopped your nose from bleeding," I said.

"I think . . . I think I got bigger problems than that," he said.

"We need to keep the blood out of the water," I said.

"Sharks smell that from far away, don't they?" Shane said.

"Yeah," I said.

"How far away can they smell it?" Shane asked.

Miles, I thought to myself.

"I don't know," I said. "Let's be on the safe side."

I got between Shane and Mr. Jordan and held onto their BCDs. I knew it was important for us to stay together. None of us wanted to be alone, and it would be easier for a boat to see us as a group.

8

I HELD ON TO THE JORDANS AND TRIED TO RELAX AND CONSERVE
my strength. I thought about the last couple of days I'd
spent with Mom. On Thursday I'd finished my finals and
felt good about all of them. The following day I spent at
home packing for the next three months. It probably takes
me longer than most people to pack. I like to organize.
Dad says I'm like Mom in this way. I get antsy when things
are out of place.

Friday evening I thought Mom would take me to dinner.
Maybe somewhere nice like Ruth's Chris Steak House.
But she didn't get home until almost eight o'clock. I was
in the living room watching television when she came

through the front door. I heard her dump her computer bag and a box of files on the kitchen counter. I got up and went to see if I could help her with anything.

I found her standing by the sink, filling a glass with water.

"Hey," I said.

She turned to me. Her hair was disheveled and her face was creased with worry lines. She leaned against the counter and sipped the water and studied me.

"Hey, sweetie," she finally said.

"Long day?"

Mom nodded. "There's been an unexpected development in my court case."

"Can you still drive me to Gulf Shores tomorrow?"

"I don't see that I have much of a choice about it," she said.

Mom set down her glass of water. Then she noticed my packed bags sitting by the front door. She looked at me and seemed to remember that I was about to be gone for the summer. She stepped over to me and turned me gently by the shoulder and began pulling the rubber band from my ponytail.

"How about we order some Chinese and then do a movie and some popcorn?" she said.

"Sounds good," I said.

She ordered takeout for us, and after eating we both

got into our pajamas and climbed into Mom's bed. I picked out a comedy and we watched it on her bedroom television. It was the first time in a long time that I remembered us laughing that much together. It was better than Ruth's Chris.

On the way down to Gulf Shores Saturday morning Mom kept her cell phone out of sight. Somehow that day, she managed to keep her mind clear of whatever was going on at work. We drove along in silence, and for the first time in a long time, I felt I could ask her questions and she could give me answers without being distracted. But all the questions I had involved Dad, and I didn't want to upset her.

"Have you called Karen yet?" she asked me.

"Not yet," I said. "But I will."

Karen was my best friend at Gulf Shores Elementary. After I first moved away she and I talked several times a week. Then only once or twice a month. And last summer she was at camp part of the time and the rest of the time I wasn't able to see her near as much as I thought I would. I knew she had new friends now, and every time I thought about her, I got a little sick feeling that maybe we'd never be as close as we used to be.

"It's kind of hard keeping friends in two places," I said.

"I know," she replied. "It's hard. It's all hard."

I didn't respond. When she said things like that it made me angry. Because it seemed to me that she could fix it all if she wanted. That it didn't have to be this hard. That it never had to be this hard.

Mom reached over and stroked my hair. "I want you to have a good summer with your father," she said. "He deserves that. It's only that I'll miss you. And I want you to be safe."

I nodded and didn't say anything.

Our old home was a modest one-level frame house in a small suburb off the canal road. As soon as we pulled into the driveway and parked behind Dad's old pickup truck, Brownie, I knew something was different. The grass was cut and Brownie had been washed. Dad hated yardwork, and I'd never known him to care about washing his truck. Even Mom was surprised.

"Well," she said, "this is certainly a change for the better."

Before she even shut off the Range Rover I saw Dad coming out the front door wiping his hands on a dishrag.

It was like he'd stepped out of the picture I'd had of him in my mind. Same old plaid shirt, cutoff khaki shorts, and flip-flops. His hair was still a wild, unmanageable mop of gray, but his smile made me feel warm all over.

I got out of the car and ran to hug him. He squeezed me like a big bear, and I breathed in the smell of him, salt and sweat and a trace of Old Spice. After a moment I pulled away and grabbed his hand and tugged him toward the Range Rover. Mom already had the back open and was reaching in for my bags. I felt Dad's hand trembling. Since their split he was always awkward and nervous around her.

"Hey, Barbara," he said.

Mom held one of my bags out to him and he took it from her. "How are you, Gib?"

"Good," he replied, and reached in for my other suitcase. "I've got this," he said.

Dad backed away with the bags while Mom shut the door.

"You want to come inside?" he asked.

Mom hesitated. "I suppose I'll stay for a minute," she said. "To help Julie get situated."

We followed Dad through the front door and into the living room. The house had not looked so clean since Mom and I had moved out two years before.

"Well, Gib, this is certainly an improvement," Mom commented.

I saw a smile appear at the edge of Dad's mouth. It was obvious he was trying to impress her, but I was a little confused about the timing of it all.

We followed him into my room. I always found it strange seeing my old pictures and toys and even the bedspread and pillows still exactly as I'd left them the year before. Dad set my bags on my bed. Then he backed away as Mom came past him.

"I'll leave you two alone," he said.

Mom helped me get unpacked. Then after a while she walked out and said some things to Dad that I couldn't hear. When I came out of my room I saw them standing side by side and imagined for a moment that they were still together. That we were all still here in the house like we used to be. But then Mom turned and looked at me, and I knew it was time for her to go.

"Okay, Julie," she said.

I walked with her out to the car.

"Be safe," was all she said.

"I will," I said.

I gave her a hug and watched her back out and drive away. I remember wanting her gone. Now I felt guilty about that and wished I'd said more to her before she left.

9

THERE'S A THING I HEARD ALL THE TIME FROM DAD ABOUT
Mother Nature. She doesn't mind you admiring her, but
she lets you know if you've gotten too close and overstayed
your welcome. And if she feels disrespected and finds you
vulnerable, stripped of all your comforts and safety, she'll
throw challenges at you. She'll make sure you don't forget for a second who's really in control. If you get too
close, you'll find she's really a very mean lady.

The waves were growing taller, and I guessed we were
bobbing and drifting in three- to four-foot swells. Not
only was it hard holding on to the Jordans, but it was
going to be difficult for Dad to see us. I took Shane's

speargun from him, removed my mask, and tied it to the tip of the spear. My mask frame was neon yellow and the best thing I had to make a sort of flag. I gave the speargun back to Shane and told him to jam the butt of it between my back and the inside of my BCD. He did so, and it was uncomfortable, but I felt better having some form of a signal above us.

I regained my grip on Shane and Mr. Jordan and the three of us floated quietly. Mr. Jordan occasionally groaned and coughed. It seemed the fabric I'd shoved into his nose was working, but the blood trickling out of his mouth was getting washed away. And I knew even those small traces of scent were trailing us, settling into the water and hanging there for cruising sharks to pull into their gills and savor and follow in their dead-eyed mechanical way.

I've read a lot about all types of sea creatures and learned even more about them from Dad. The main problem with sharks is that they're unpredictable. They don't think in a way we can comprehend. Most people like to relate all big fish to porpoises and whales, but those are mammals and there's a big difference. Even the most predatory marine mammals, like killer whales, seem to have some trace of compassion. You see it in the wet depths of their eyes, as if the eyes connect directly to their brain and give you a window into their feelings. A person can look into eyes like that and think they have some chance to connect and communicate. Sharks are fish, an entirely different thing. Like with snakes and other reptiles, fish eyes never show pain or stress or longing. They're like marbles connected not to the brain, but to the mouth—they simply guide the mouth to food and nothing more.

Sharks' eyes are even more sinister. They are narrow and black, huge night-vision pupils that orient in a vertical slit and reflect in the dark like a cat's. On many of our overnight trips on the *Barbie Doll* we've watched these reflections moving in large patrolling circles below us.

"They don't think," Dad told me once. "They just kill and eat."

Dad's also the one who told me they don't feel pain. He said he watched a feeding frenzy once when he was a deckhand on a billfishing charter. A swarm of sharks was feeding on a whale carcass. They were buried into the whale and snapping and tearing at it like a pack of crazed dogs. They were so bunched up and mad with the smell of blood that they often tore into each other by mistake. He saw one of the sharks with its stomach completely ripped out, still feeding for another few minutes until the life suddenly left it. Then he watched the body go limp and slowly sink away. A moment later several other sharks noticed, darted down to it, and ripped it up even more and ate it.

Compared to getting in a car wreck or even getting struck by lightning, shark attacks are rare. But not many people find themselves floating for hours in open water. If a shark finds you and you hang before its face long enough, I can't imagine it not wanting to take a bite. They're not scared of anything. How can you be scared when you don't feel pain? And once that bite draws blood, they've found what they were looking for and they can't stop themselves from tearing you to pieces.

By all my reasoning it was only a matter of time before sharks found us. And then they would certainly kill us.

"What's taking your dad so long?" Shane said.

I turned to him and said, "I don't know."

He looked at his dad. Mr. Jordan stared back and blinked helplessly. I thought of how I would feel if I were in the same situation with my own dad. I'd certainly be frantic with worry. I could never stand to see him like that. But I didn't detect any sympathy on Shane's part. And it didn't seem like Mr. Jordan expected any.

I looked at my watch. Nearly an hour and a half had passed since I'd surfaced. We'd been floating together for close to an hour.

Mr. Jordan sputtered and coughed again. I studied

him and saw that he was having a hard time holding his head up and his empty tank was floating high in the water.

"Let's ditch the tanks and regulators," I said.

"Why?" Shane asked.

"It'll be easier to float."

"We just got these things."

I grew frustrated with him again but outwardly kept my cool.

"Do what you want," I said. "Mine and your dad's are coming off."

I got around behind Mr. Jordan and unclipped and disconnected his pony tank first. As I pulled it away I noticed that it wanted to sink. Despite what most people think, air weighs something. A full tank will sink while an empty tank will float. I grabbed the valve and turned it. Gas hissed from the nozzle. Apparently Mr. Jordan had air the entire time. He wasn't hurt because he ran out of air; he was hurt because he panicked and became so confused that he turned the tank off instead of on. And none of it would have happened had he not stayed down too long and been greedy about spearing fish.

Shane hadn't noticed my discovery. I was about to let the pony tank go when I had another idea. I reconnected it to Mr. Jordan's BCD. Then I disconnected his main tank and shoved it aside to drift away. Finally I put the regulator from the pony tank into his mouth.

"Breath on that," I said. "It'll keep the waves from splashing into your mouth."

I heard the regulator click and hiss as Mr. Jordan began taking breaths.

"I thought it was empty," Shane said.

"It's not," I said, unclipping my own hoses and turning my back to him. "Take mine off."

After he had it free I grabbed my gauge console before the floating tank dragged it away. I popped out the compass module and shoved it into the pocket of my BCD.

"What about my pony tank?" Shane said. "I've still got a little air in it."

"Lose it," I said. "It's making you more tired."

He hesitated, but after a moment he began unfastening everything and turned his back to me so that I could get the tank off.

Then we were all floating easier and things became quiet again except for the rolling of the waves and the steady click and hiss of Mr. Jordan's regulator.

"How much is in there?" Shane finally asked.

"It's full," I said.

10

I STARED AT THE BLUE SKY, SQUINTING AGAINST THE SUN, FEELING it beat down on my face. My eyes caught flashes of a tiny reflective dot high overhead. It was a small plane so far away that I couldn't even hear it. This made me consider how improbable it was, with all of our technology, that I could have found myself so completely out of touch, and how quickly it had happened. All because we broke our number-one rule about dive trips: If it doesn't feel right for any reason, don't go down.

There were so many reasons it hadn't felt right, but so many reasons it had to be done. Most of all, Dad was broke and needed the money. I should have known that his efforts to clean up around the house were only an attempt to cover much bigger issues he didn't want Mom to know about.

It was hard to imagine that his dive business had gotten so bad in the nine months I'd been gone. The parking lot was tall with weeds, and there was barely any scuba equipment for sale on the shelves. Then yesterday I found the unpaid mortgage statements buried under a pile of bills on his desk. I'd already spent last summer helping him run the place. I knew what those statements were and what they meant.

"Business has been slow, Julie," he said defensively. "It happens."

"Dad," I said in disbelief, "there are *fourteen* unanswered messages on the answering machine."

"You see," he said cheerfully, "it's not so bad."

His carefree attitude didn't make me feel better at all. It only made me angry. We both knew this had nothing to do with slow business. It was all about him finding the Malzon tanks. I knew Dad had been distracted, but I never imagined he'd let his obsession almost ruin his business.

"What if the tanks don't have any fish on them yet?"

"They've got fish," he said confidently.

"How do you know?"

"Because I was out there three days ago."

"And you went down? And saw for yourself?"

"I only got to twenty feet, but I could see them. Swarming it like bees."

I took a deep breath, feeling my anxiety over it all slowly ease.

"Then start calling those people back," I said. "We need to book some trips."

"I thought we'd dive it together first. Tomorrow. Sort of a celebration."

I felt frustration grip me again. "I'll be here all summer, Dad. And I'm not going to enjoy myself until we get some trips booked, clean this place up, and pay the bills."

"Well, if that's how you feel, sweetheart. Hand me the phone and let's make some calls."

I thrust the handset out to him. "I can't believe I'm even having to tell you this," I said.

"Who's the first person on the machine?" he asked.

"Forget the older ones for now," I said. "You can call them back and apologize later. Mr. Jordan's last message was yesterday. He might be your only chance at someone who hasn't already made other plans."

"God," he said. "Hank's such a pain."

"So is his son, Shane," I said. "But at this point we'll take what we can get."

"Fine." Dad sighed. "Give me his number."

I sat at the desk and replayed the last of Mr. Jordan's three increasingly angry messages. Then I wrote the number on a Post-it note and gave it to Dad.

"My business partner's back in town," he joked.

11

THE SUN BEAT DOWN ON US. MY HEAD WAS COOKING AND MY eyes stung with salt. The speargun felt like a stick stabbing me in the back, and no matter how I shifted there was little relief. Worst of all, my mouth was dry and I was overcome with a terrible thirst. I couldn't stop thinking about pouring ice-cold fresh water down my throat.

"We've been drifting for almost two hours," Shane said.

"He'll find us unless something went wrong," I said.

"How can he have any idea where we are?"

I looked at Shane. I could see he was on the verge of panic again.

"Because all he has to do is follow the current."

"Then where is he? We're gonna die out here!"

I decided it was time to start lying. Being honest wasn't going to work anymore. "This kind of thing happens all the time," I said. "He probably had engine trouble. He'll fix it and get here as fast as he can."

Shane spit salt water from his mouth. "This doesn't happen all the time! It never happens!"

Actually, it did. Divers get separated from their boats more than people think. But I was tired of arguing.

Shane continued on his rant. "First the stupid anchor pulls and then the boat breaks. I told Dad this was the biggest joke of a dive shop around. You'll be lucky if he doesn't sue you."

"Your dad's an idiot for staying down so long. He ought to be more concerned with his life than with suing people!"

"We paid your dad a ton of money for that dive. More money than he deserves for some crappy boat that breaks down."

"You're a jerk, Shane."

"Just do something, will you! God, I'm so thirsty."

I locked eyes with him and shook his shoulder strap. "Don't you drink this seawater."

"I know. Everybody knows that."

His mouth was trembling. I realized that we were both

just scared, but it was coming out like anger. I looked away. "Good," I said. "Then shut up and calm down. There's nothing I can do."

Shane spit again.

"I'm thirsty, too, you know," I said.

He didn't answer me.

"You think I want to be out here? Stop whining to me."

"Or what? You going to punch me in the face again?"

"Just shut up, will you, Shane?"

Mr. Jordan coughed and I looked at him. His pony tank had run out and his regulator was trailing behind.

"What's wrong, Dad?" Shane asked.

"I can feel my arms," he said.

"You're probably getting better," Shane said. "What about your legs?"

Mr. Jordan shook his head.

From what I knew about the bends, I could tell he wasn't getting better. Maybe he was experiencing some temporary relief, but the bends doesn't fix itself. In fact, I suspected he had more than the bends. Dad had told me about people's lungs collapsing. And he'd said they'll usually bleed out of their mouth and nose when this happens.

I reached behind myself and jerked the speargun from my back. I shoved Shane sideways and got behind him.

"What are you doing?"

I jammed the butt of the gun down the back of his BCD.

"Owww!" he yelped.

"Your turn," I said.

12

ABOUT TWO-THIRTY THAT AFTERNOON CLOUDS BEGAN TO GATHER overhead. I was never so happy to see the glare of the sun disappear. We hadn't spoken a word in almost an hour. I didn't even want to look at Shane, but the few times I did I saw his face pink and swollen from sunburn.

Shane eventually broke the silence. "Maybe the boat sank."

"The boat didn't sink," I said.

"The anchor pulled. Your dad should have drifted the same speed as us even if he was broken down. He would have been down-current. Right?" he asked.

"Right," I mumbled.

"So what could be the problem?"

"If the boat sank, there'd still be stuff floating all around us. Don't be stupid."

"If it didn't sink, there'd be a boat here *getting* us."

I didn't answer him. He wasn't telling me anything I hadn't thought about. And I didn't like not having answers.

"I want a Coke," he said. "With crushed ice."

"Shut up."

"I want to lie in a bucket of ice water."

"Your dad might want you to help him to the hospital first."

Shane looked at his father. "He knows what I mean."

I grabbed Shane's wrist and brought his hand to the shoulder strap of my BCD.

"Hold on to me," I said.

I was surprised he didn't complain. I felt his fingers slip under the strap and grip it. I let go of him and pulled the compass module from my pocket and studied it. We were still moving southeast, but it was hard to tell how fast. Then I remembered the small bottom marker in my pocket. It was nothing more than a red cork with a hundred and fifty feet of thin monofilament line wrapped around it. If you tied the line to something on the seafloor and let it go it would unravel and rise to the top, discreetly marking a place you wanted to revisit later.

I pulled Mr. Jordan to me and swung him toward Shane.

"Hold on to your dad with your other arm," I said.

"Why?"

"So I can use my hands."

Shane took him and I got out the marker and clamped it in my mouth. I reached over and unclipped Mr. Jordan's empty pony tank. I disconnected the regulator and let the tank drift away. Then I got my dive knife and cut the air hoses from the heavy metal hardware that connects to the tank nozzle.

"What are you doing?"

"Measuring," I replied.

I took the marker from my mouth and tied the end of the string to what was left of the regulator and dropped it, letting the line spool in my hands. After nearly a minute the line stopped and I tied off the cork. Then I measured out another twenty feet, noted the position of the second hand of my watch, and let go.

I counted to ten before the slack between me and the cork was taken.

"Ten seconds," I said aloud. "That's two feet per second."

"So what?"

"So there's three thousand six hundred seconds in an hour. Two times three thousand six hundred is . . . seven thousand two hundred. There's five thousand two hundred and eighty feet in a mile. Seven thousand two hundred divided by five thousand two hundred and eighty is ... about one and a half. So we're moving at about one and a half miles per hour to the southeast."

"That's not very fast," he said.

"Maybe not in a car, but you left the bottom at about ten-forty-five, which means we've been drifting for almost four hours. We're nearly six miles from where we started."

"So what happens if we keep going?"

"We might see some fishermen."

"But no land?"

"It would take a long time to get back to land."

"How long?"

I didn't want to answer him. I didn't want him freaking out. "I don't know," I said.

"Guess," he said. "If we kept drifting?"

"We're not going toward land," I said. "We're headed out."

"Out to where?"

I began reeling up the marker. "Out," I said, "to blue water."

Shane didn't ask what blue water was. Nearly eighty miles offshore, the emerald-green inland waters of the Gulf meet the jade-blue of deep oceanic water. The two don't mix; instead, they collide to form a distinct wavering wall that goes straight down for hundreds of feet. Giant fish travel along it: tuna, blue marlin, and swordfish—fish that prefer the clarity, depth, and purity of the blue zone and travel its border like beasts against a fence. It is truly the place where monsters lurk.

I had never been there, but I'd heard Dad talk about it and I'd pulled up pictures of it on the Internet. I'd always wanted to go, but not like this. Now it was the last thing I ever wanted to see.

13

THE HOURS PASSED WITH EACH OF US LOST IN OUR OWN SILENT thoughts, fighting thirst and frustration. We saw no birds, no fish, no planes, no sign of life except for each other. In the distance a storm hung on the horizon, occasionally grumbling rumbles of thunder.

"My neck itches," Shane said, scratching himself.

"Sea lice," I said.

"What's that?"

"Baby jellyfish."

"This sucks," he said.

"It'll get worse."

Shane sighed. "Do we still need the flag?"

"I'll take it for a while," I said.

I pulled the speargun off his back and gave it to him. Then I turned and winced as he shoved it into place on my back.

"Maybe it'll rain," I said.

"If I could only let a little rainwater touch my tongue," he said. "It feels like a dried rag."

"It doesn't help to talk about it," I said.

Shane turned toward his father. "Dad?" he said.

Mr. Jordan didn't answer. He had his eyes closed, but he still coughed occasionally.

"Dad, how do you feel?"

Mr. Jordan nodded slowly.

"Don't talk to him," I said. "He doesn't feel like talking."

Shane glared at me. "Nobody's coming," he said. "And it's going to be dark soon."

"The Coast Guard can search at night."

"Not if they don't know we're out here," he said.

"Look, there's no way they won't come looking for us. Somebody's going to figure out we're gone. What time did your mom expect you back?"

"She doesn't even know we went," he said.

"You didn't tell her?"

"She's in Bermuda. We have a house there."

I felt my sense of hopelessness grow even more sickening.

"What about *your* mom?" he said.

"My parents are divorced. She's in Atlanta. She knows we were going diving but nothing about when we'd be back or where we went."

Shane sighed. "This sucks. Man, this sucks."

"She could be trying to call me, but she knows cell phones don't work this far out. And sometimes we spend the night anchored up."

"Something happened to your dad, Julie."

It was strange to hear Shane say my name. It was the first time I could remember him using it.

"Before we got in the water he said he wasn't feeling well."

"He's got diabetes," I said. "That's all it was. He was queasy."

"Maybe he couldn't find us," Shane continued. "And he radioed the Coast Guard and it's taking them a while to get their search organized."

"Yeah," I said. "It's probably just taking them a while."

I'd already thought about every possible scenario concerning the boat, but nothing made sense. It wouldn't simply sink. Not that fast. It wouldn't have exploded from gas fumes in the engine compartment or we'd have found pieces of it. I wasn't ready to accept that something had happened to Dad, but it was the only scenario that made sense.

No matter how sick he was, he would have called the Coast Guard. Unless he'd fallen overboard . . . Unless he tried to reset the anchor by himself, fell over, and drowned. Then the Barbie Doll *would still be anchored somewhere close to the tanks. And the boat was empty with a raised dive flag. And no one would think to stop and check on it.*

"Queen of diamonds, ace high," Mr. Jordan mumbled.

Both of us looked at him. He still had his eyes closed.

"What'd you say, Dad?"

Mr. Jordan didn't answer. A moment later he mumbled something else we couldn't understand.

"He's not making sense," I said. "He's talking to himself."

"He likes to gamble," Shane said.

I looked at Shane. He had a strange look on his face, like he'd just realized something horrible.

"I think he's about to die," he said.

I started to disagree, but stopped myself. "Keep holding on to him," I said.

14

THE SUN SET BELOW THE HORIZON, BEHIND THE STORM THAT rumbled and pulsed with lightning. I dropped the marker again, made my calculations, and shoved the spool back into my pocket. Then I checked my compass. We were still drifting to the southeast, but slower now. And I started to question why I was even bothering with navigation. There was no chance we were going to survive in the water long enough to get to land. But it was something to break the monotony. To make me stop thinking that the worst was yet to come.

"You want me to take the flag for a while?" Shane asked.

I was tired of pretending things were going to be okay. I didn't have the energy to both try to survive and make him feel better about our situation.

"I don't care," I said.

"You think it even matters?"

"I don't know."

"It's almost dark," Shane said. "I don't see why we need it now."

"Take it out," I said. "I'll hold it."

Shane pulled the speargun out of my BCD. It felt so good to lose that bulky rod down my spine. I worked my shoulders in a circle and loosened up my bruised and tight back muscles. I saw Shane studying his dad.

"What do you think?" I said.

"It doesn't even seem like I know him," he said. "He works all the time."

"My mom does the same thing," I said.

Shane grew quiet for a moment. "How long do you think we have?" he said.

"How am I supposed to know?"

"You know more than I do about survival out here," he said.

"Are you talking about dying? I'm not planning on dying."

"How long can we go without drinking water?"

"You hear that thunder? You see that storm? We're

80

headed right toward it. We'll have all the rainwater we want."

"What about the lightning?"

I looked at him. "Do you really want me to tell you what I'm worried about? Do you really want to know?"

Shane nodded skeptically.

"Fine," I said. "I'm worried about lightning. I'm worried about sharks. I'm worried about hypothermia."

Shane took a deep, nervous breath. "But you don't think we'll die?"

"And I'm worried about dying."

The Gulf water turned black with the onset of nightfall. We saw no stars, no moon, no light at all overhead except for the approaching storm that flashed like a glowing jellyfish in the sky. The waves were growing taller, and each time we rose onto a crest I felt a strong wind against my face.

For a while it seemed we might never reach the storm, but I was certain we were getting closer by the minute. And soon the thunder was no longer a faraway rumble, but an explosion I felt in my chest followed by an electric crack of light I felt in my teeth. The lightning flashes lit up the black surface like they were searching for something.

"What do we do?" Shane asked me over the building noise of the storm.

"Hold on," I said. "Don't let go of your dad. I won't let go of you."

The wind howled across the tops of the waves, white-capping them and rolling them over us. There was so much spray already pounding our faces that it was hard to tell when the rain started. I noticed Mr. Jordan turning sideways, coughing water.

"Spin him around!" I shouted over the noise. "Keep his back to the waves!"

"I can't! He keeps turning!"

"Get him between us!"

We swam around until we had Mr. Jordan squeezed between us. After only a few seconds I realized how hard it was to steer his limp weight and keep myself positioned at the same time. And suddenly I was angry at him again.

You tried to kill us once and now you're trying to kill us again. Why can't you go ahead and die?

I knew it was really just as much Dad's fault that we were in this situation, but Mr. Jordan was easier to dislike and a lot easier to blame. I couldn't let go of him, but I was starting to think that maybe I should only be concerned with myself. After all, if it wasn't for the Jordans we'd never be out here. If Mr. Jordan hadn't left me and gone down the anchor rope in such a hurry, I could have told them to resurface and we could have reset.

The rain started coming down harder and we saw it slanting sideways in the blue flashes of lightning. At the wave crests it stung our faces like blown sand, and even the little bit that found its way into the edges of my mouth was tantalizing as my tongue sponged it up. It was all I could do not to open my mouth and bite at it.

I looked at Shane and saw him with his head tilted back and his mouth open.

"Don't do it!" I yelled.

He rolled his eyes at me with his mouth still gaping wide.

"There's too much spray!"

He closed his mouth and stared with a look of desperation.

"Wait!" I yelled.

A contorted look of agony came over him and he rolled his head and coughed and nodded and it looked like he was crying.

The air exploded like someone slamming a steel door, and lightning blinded my eyes like a thousand camera flashes in my face. The water went from black to a deep translucent blue and I saw suspended jellyfish glowing in the depths. I clenched my teeth and braced myself for an electric shock, but felt only the embrace of cold water.

Another explosion, the blinding light so close that it felt like we were inside it, and I couldn't even tell where it was, penetrating the rain-tattered swells like a flashlight dropped into a bathtub. I heard Shane yell and I looked at him. He was hugging his father, clamped to him like he'd crawl inside him if he could. I wanted to yell, too, but something told me that if we floated quietly maybe the storm wouldn't see us. Maybe it'd sweep past us and move off into the night, searching for someone else.

The light exploded and flashed again and I drew my knees up and shut my eyes and braced myself. I felt the energy of it like ice on my teeth. Then I realized that if I was considering it at all, I must still be alive. That its electric fingers hadn't found me yet. Shane yelled again and I saw him squeezing his dad tighter. Suddenly I didn't want to be alone, tossed about and exposed at arm's length. I pulled myself close to Mr. Jordan and hugged his back.

15

THE STORM RUMBLED PAST, LEAVING THE WATER BEATEN INTO high, smooth swells. We caught the rain in our mouths and held out our masks to collect more. It took a few minutes to catch a quarter inch, not nearly enough to satisfy our craving, but enough to give us hope and to make us believe that we were going to survive a little bit longer.

To our surprise Mr. Jordan was able to move his arms enough to hold one of the masks of water and tilt it to his lips. It seemed we were all so happy to be alive that we'd found new energy. Mr. Jordan drank silently and then I gave him his own mask and propped his hands near his chin so that he could collect water.

"Please keep raining," Shane said to himself.

I was thinking the same thing.

"Just no more thunderstorms," he said. "I thought we were dead."

I drank what was in my mask again and held it out for more.

"You need some help, Dad?" Shane asked.

Mr. Jordan shook his head. He lifted, tilted, and sipped.

"Did you see all the jellyfish?" Shane said. "They were everywhere."

"Yeah," I said.

"I wonder if the lightning kills any fish?"

"I hear they go deep," I said. "I think they know."

"Man," Shane said. "I don't see how it gets scarier than that."

It was the scariest thing I'd ever experienced, but I knew things could get worse.

Sharks, I thought. *Lightning is nothing compared to sharks.*

In the early-morning hours the rain stopped and the Gulf was calm and still. I found myself nodding off, so I cut three short lengths of line from the marker spool and used one to tie the speargun to my waist. Then I gave Shane one and told him to tie himself to his dad on one side and I would do the same on the other. We connected ourselves loosely so that we couldn't be separated by more than eight or ten feet if we drifted apart.

I told Shane to try to sleep before the sun came up and while the seas still lay in a post-storm calm. Then I shut my eyes and drifted off.

Light came against my eyelids and I opened them to see the sun, cool and orange, peeking above the eastern horizon. Like it had been looking for us all night and was now coming back again.

"Where do you think we are?" Shane asked.

I looked at him. Like me, he was no longer holding on to Mr. Jordan but drifting a few feet away.

I took out the marker and dropped the regulator. This time it took a lot longer and spooled nearly all the line. My calculations revealed the current to be about two miles per hour, still to the southeast.

"Drifting faster," I said. "But it's too complicated to figure out. That storm could have blown us in another direction. And I don't know when the current sped up."

"Guess," he said.

"Fifty miles, maybe," I said. "It's too hard to know. But we should be reaching blue water soon."

"What's that?"

"The water will turn clear and blue as a swimming pool. It's where you go to catch billfish and tuna. Deep water. Hundreds and even thousands of feet deep."

"Is that bad?"

"I don't know. I've never seen it. But I've heard about it."

"There's no way they won't find us today," Shane said. "Dad won't show at work, and they'll know we're missing for sure."

"I can't believe we haven't seen anything," I said. "No search planes. No ships. Not even a fisherman."

"I hope they hurry up and get here. I don't think I can take another day in the sun. My face feels like a big scab and my lips are cracked."

"We're going to need some more water," I said.

"How?" he asked.

"And we have to figure a way to keep from getting so sunburned."

"There's nothing we can do," he said.

"We need to take off our skinsuits. We can wrap them around our heads."

"I'm too cold."

"You do what you want," I said. "I'm taking mine off."

I swam close to Shane and gave him the speargun and my fins. Then I worked myself out of the BCD and passed that to him, too. He watched as I held my breath and struggled underwater to get out of my wetsuit. When I finally had it free I balled it before me and floated on it in nothing but my skinsuit. I felt the cool salt water caress my skin and considered the consequences of what I'd done. The sea lice would soon be trapped inside my wetsuit and feeling like flea bites. But they would have gotten inside eventually. I was just speeding up the process.

After I caught my breath I told Shane to turn around. It felt tiresome and silly being modest in such a situation, but I wasn't going to strip naked in front of him.

Shane turned away. When I was sure he wasn't looking I put the wetsuit in my teeth, went under, and peeled off the skinsuit. Then I surfaced, hugged the wetsuit to me, and caught my breath again. Shane was still looking away and Mr. Jordan had his eyes closed.

"Don't even think about turning around," I said.

"I'm not!" he said.

Once I got into my wetsuit again I swam to him and grabbed my BCD.

"Are you done?" he asked.

"Yes," I said. "I'm done. You can turn around."

He watched while I got into my BCD and slipped my fins back on.

"That couldn't have been easy," he said.

"It wasn't," I replied. "Don't try it. I might be able to cut enough fabric from my skinsuit for all of us. Besides, yours is black and it might get too hot."

When I was floating again I took out my knife and began cutting the legs and arms off the skinsuit. Then I cut out two eye holes and a mouth slit into one of the legs and gave it to Shane.

"Pull it over your face and see how it does."

He did. It was tight but looked like it would work.

"Not bad," he said.

I made another one and told him to pull it over his dad's face. Finally, I tried to fit a sleeve over my own head but it was too small. I cut slits in the torso section and found it to fit much better.

I heard Mr. Jordan mumbling something as Shane worked with him.

"It's all right, Dad," Shane said. "It's to keep the sun off."

I saw Mr. Jordan fumbling his hands over his face, making it difficult. Shane finally managed to get the cloth over his head and position the holes so that his eyes blinked back at us, dull and crazed.

"Leave it on," Shane said to him.

The man's hands slowly sank to his sides again. Either he understood or didn't have the energy to fight the mask. I put the knife up and considered my two companions. I thought we made a strange sight, like bank robbers dropped into the ocean from above.

16

AS THE SUN CLIMBED HIGHER IN THE SKY IT SEEMED TO FOCUS all of its heat directly on our heads. I felt I'd won a small victory with the skinsuit masks, but I knew that nothing we did was a permanent fix. I was starting to believe that none of my defenses really mattered anymore. My exposed skin below the water was soggy white and as dead-looking as cadaver meat. It felt like the sea lice were eating it from my bones. And if my outside environment wasn't enough to finish me off, dehydration was attacking me from the inside, leaving my mouth and throat swollen. The agonizing pain, both mental and physical, was like nothing I'd ever felt or imagined.

"I got kicked out of school," I heard Shane say.

After a moment I said, "What?"

"I got kicked out of school," he repeated.

I wasn't sure why he was telling me this, but it didn't cross my mind to have any sympathy for him.

"What'd you do?"

"I got caught cheating. Twice. On my final exams."

I wasn't surprised.

"Now I'm going to boarding school," he continued.

"Well, you can start over then."

"I guess so," he said.

"You don't have any friends, do you?"

"Yeah, I have friends," he said defensively.

"Like who?" I challenged.

"Nobody you know. You don't even live here anymore."

"How can you have friends when you act like a spoiled brat?"

"You think I act like a spoiled brat?"

"Are you kidding? You argue with your dad over who gets the newest speargun. There's people who would work all summer to have your *old* dive equipment."

"He drives me crazy. Nothing I do is good enough for him."

"What's that got to do with it? I don't understand why you wouldn't want to be nice to people. Why would you want to be a jerk?"

"I wish you'd stop calling me that."

"Fine," I said. "I'm sorry for calling you names."

"And I got the coordinates of the Malzon tanks on my iPhone."

I turned and faced him. "See, you're a total jerk, Shane! You know how long and hard my dad worked to find those tanks? You know how much he gave up for that?"

"I—"

"He wrecked our family over those things! And you think you can steal it all on his first trip out? Just when he was finally heading in the right direction. You're hopeless!"

"It was—"

"You and your dad both deserve whatever you've got coming. And it really sucks that I've got to go down with you."

"It was a mistake," he said.

"Oh, *now* it is. I'm sure it's all a mistake *now*. Now that I'm the only one who can save your butt. Yep, here I am. The girl who was going to bring up your fish. Shut up and don't talk to me."

"I didn't have to tell you," he said.

I lifted my arm and made a fist and held it before him. "Shut up!" I warned.

The sun was directly overhead, hot and getting hotter, while my body from the neck down was cold and getting colder. None of us were talking, and Mr. Jordan even appeared to be sleeping. Time passed like there was no real system to it at all, like it was something you imagined, something that Mother Nature could slow down and use to torture us.

I heard a splashing to my right. I turned to rest my eyes on a sea turtle that must have been five feet across. It flipped its way easily along the surface, not the least bit alarmed by us.

"Is it dangerous?" Shane asked.

I didn't answer him.

I thought about the turtle and how comfortable it was way out here in this desolate landscape. There was nothing it could do for us, but it made me feel better to finally see something else alive. And the turtle was a connection with land. Perhaps it had even been born on the beach in Gulf Shores.

"Got any news, Mr. Turtle?" I said.

It came slowly past me, so close I reached out and

touched its soft, leathery shell. Then I had a strange thought. Maybe, way out here where no one would ever know, it might talk to me. Maybe all of nature's creatures really could communicate with us, but didn't. They let us believe we were so smart and watched us and laughed at us. And only when we were about to die would this big trick be revealed.

"Talk to us," I said.

"You're losing it," Shane mumbled.

"Shut up, Shane," I said.

The turtle paddled away and loneliness and misery settled over me again. The thirst was the worst of it all. So bad that I started to think about drowning. How it might be the best way to go. Nothing, I decided, could be worse than being thirsty. But a small voice inside me reasoned that if I was facing death I might as well fight it. There was really nothing to lose. The end result was all the same.

17

ACCORDING TO MY DIVE WATCH, IT WAS TWO O'CLOCK IN THE afternoon when we reached blue water. The wall was so defined that I could float on the green side of it and stick my hand through into the blue. It was enormous and remote and as frightening as something from outer space. The current was going to pull us beyond it no matter what we did, but the wall was no place I wanted to linger.

I began swimming until I felt the tug of my companions against the line behind me.

"Get away from it," I said.

The tone of my voice was enough to keep Shane from

asking questions. He tugged his father and followed me out of the green and into the blue swells.

After a few minutes I stopped and rested.

"What'd you see?" he said.

"Nothing," I said. "I just didn't like it."

"What makes the water so different out here? Why the blue?"

"There's more particles in the green. It reflects the light differently."

"If we had a map, where would this be?"

"Somewhere between Alabama and the Florida peninsula. It moves."

"The line moves?"

"Yeah, it moves with the tide and current. Can you stop asking questions?"

"There's got to be fishermen out here," he said, ignoring me. "There's got to be somebody, right?"

I didn't answer him.

"I'm itching all over. I think those sea lice are in my wetsuit. Are they eating me?"

I hoped they were. When I didn't respond Shane turned to me. He watched me, but I wouldn't look at him.

"Dad told me to get those coordinates, Julie. It wasn't my idea."

"I don't care anymore," I said. "Stop talking."

"It's just us now. I don't want to die like this."

He had a point. If anything, it was tiresome being angry. Tiresome and senseless in the face of what we were up against.

"No," I said. "They're not eating you."

"They're driving me crazy."

I finally turned to him. "I don't understand how your dad being a jerk gives you an excuse to be one," I said.

"I think I'm mad at him all the time. And it makes me mad at everybody else. The reason I'm never good enough for him is that I just cost him money."

I looked at Mr. Jordan. There was no sign he heard us talking about him.

"Money sucks," I said.

"So you know what I mean?"

"In a different way. My parents are messed up over trying to make it. Yours are messed up over trying to spend it."

"Is that why they got divorced?"

"I don't know, really. Sometimes I think that if Dad was any good at making money, then Mom would have been happier. But now Mom's making a lot of money and she seems more unhappy than ever."

"And then you die and it doesn't mean anything."

"Nope."

"And maybe we could have been friends," he said.

I shook my head. "You really are clueless."

"What?"

"Us being friends has nothing to do with whether or not either of us has money. You have to care about somebody besides yourself. You're not nice."

"Well, you're the one who punches people in the face. What's with you and the attitude?"

I looked at him. "What's with you and your stupid long hair?"

He stared back at me with the ridiculous mask over his face. I imagined his look saying *But you can't even see my hair.* And it was all suddenly funny to me.

I began to laugh uncontrollably, and a moment later Shane was laughing with me.

"You look like something out of a bad homemade horror movie," I said. "Like an iPhone horror movie."

"I can be nice," he finally said.

"Okay, when's the last time you were nice?"

"We took a field trip to a nursing home before school let out. I met this old lady and played bingo with her."

"What was her name?"

"Well, I don't remember."

"So she's just *Old Lady*?"

"I played *bingo* with her!" he said defensively. "And I knew her name at the time. But I don't remember it now."

I chuckled. "Okay. At least you have a little bit of heart."

We drifted along without speaking for a few minutes.

Then Shane said something else. "I cried when my grandfather died."

I looked at him.

"I stayed in my room for a week and wouldn't come out."

"You must have really liked him."

"He was the nicest person I ever knew. Dad never got along with him, so we didn't see him much. But sometimes he'd drive down from White Hill in his old pickup and get me, and we'd spend the day together."

"My grandparents are dead," I said. "I wish I'd known them."

"I called him Papa. He didn't have a lot of money, but I never felt better than when I was with him. He loved to fish more than anything, but he always took me to the movies instead."

"Why?"

"Because he knew it was what *I* wanted to do, not what *he* wanted to do. And then we'd go out for some cheap Mexican food and talk about the movies and what we thought of them."

"Why didn't they get along?"

Shane looked at his father. "I think Dad was ashamed."

"Of what?"

Shane turned to me again.

"Of growing up poor," he said. "Of having a dad who worked at a service station."

Plenty of times I'd found myself frustrated with my own dad, but I was never ashamed of him.

"I thought one day I could be a lawyer," Shane said. "And then he'd be proud of me."

"It's not worth it," I said.

"It's got to be. He's the only friend I've got."

I started to make a snide comment about Shane admitting that he really didn't have any friends after all, but something in his voice made me keep quiet. I looked down past my fins at the blue water descending in bent sunbeams into the blackness of unimaginable depths. I thought of how small and whiny our problems seemed in comparison.

18

I FELT SOMETHING ROUGH BRUSH AGAINST MY LEG. I YELPED AND jerked it away instinctively.

"What?" Shane asked.

Before I even lowered my head, I knew. Underneath me I saw the sleek gray body gliding below.

So they're here. To finish us off.

My mind raced, remembering everything I'd learned about shark defense. I'd listened to Dad talk about sharks. I'd seen hundreds of them from the *Barbie Doll*. I'd even encountered a few up close on dives, but I'd never had to defend myself against one. The sharks I'd seen underwater were always curious at first, circling and inspecting us. There were mostly black tips, but occasionally we'd see nurse and bull sharks. Dad would signal to surface immediately and get into the boat before they had a chance to get aggressive.

I swam to Shane and grabbed him and Mr. Jordan.

"We've got to huddle up," I said. "Facing out."

Shane resisted. "What?" he asked again.

"Shark," I said, shoving him. "Turn around. Lock arms with me and your dad."

We locked elbows and formed a tight triangle. I held the speargun across my chest and felt myself trembling. Mr. Jordan mumbled something that I couldn't understand.

"Shoot it with the speargun," Shane said.

"Be quiet," I said.

"How many?"

"I only saw one. It bumped me."

"I'll bet there's more," he said. "There's always more."

"Stop talking," I said.

I yanked off the sun mask and stuffed it into a pocket on the front of my BCD. Then I slipped my diving mask on, gathered my courage, and lowered my face into the water. I looked around and saw nothing.

"Is it gone?" Shane said. "Tell me it's gone."

I didn't answer him. I kept searching. Then I saw it

again, a dull gray sliver far below, circling, contemplating us. Contemplating a lot of things.

Sharks only have two small blind spots, one in front of their snouts and one directly behind their heads. The way their catlike eyes are positioned on their heads gives them nearly a 360-degree view. Dad said they see the world like a black-and-white IMAX movie, considering everything that moves on the big screen a possible meal.

Shane suddenly kicked out and shouted, "Crap!"

I jerked my head around and looked at him.

"I s-saw it," he stammered. "I almost touched it with my fin."

I put my face into the water again and saw another gray sliver directly below us. This shark looked to be nearly eight feet long.

"It's another one," I told him. "Put your mask on and watch them. Kick for the snout or the gills."

"I can't kick out with the fins," he said.

"You're right," I said. "Take them off, but don't lose them. Stuff yours down my back, and I'll stuff mine down yours."

We quickly struggled with our fins until we had them free and jammed down where we'd held the speargun. Mr. Jordan wasn't going to be any help, so we were just going to have to drag him about and look after him and us at the same time.

"I'm getting my knife out," Shane said.

"Don't touch your knife," I snapped. "If you cut our BCDs by mistake we're dead."

"We're already dead," he replied.

I felt the same way, but I didn't want to admit it. It was all I could do to remain calm. Fear hummed in my ears and I felt it in my jaw. I wanted to scream against the impulse to draw myself into a ball and give up.

"Don't get out your knife," I said again. "Kick them. They're only curious right now. Sometimes they'll leave."

Shane didn't agree with me, but he didn't reach for his knife either. He took off his sun mask and put it in his BCD pocket. Then he got his dive mask over his face, locked arms with me and his dad again, and peered into the water. There was another one now. Three sharks circling not twenty feet below us, more than we could keep our eyes on. The largest of them had a scar on its side like something had bitten a chunk out of it. The other two looked like twins.

"I see three," Shane said.

I didn't answer him. I swung the speargun out and held it before me. It wasn't cocked, but I reasoned if I could poke them in the face with the sharp point it would alarm them more than a blunt kick. They looked like bull sharks, but to me, all sharks were basically the same, and knowing what kind they were wasn't going to help us.

The shark with the scar broke circle and swam out of my vision.

"Where's that one going?" Shane said. "Crap! Where's he going?"

"Look for him," I said. "I'll keep watching these other two."

Suddenly Mr. Jordan grunted, and I spun to see Scar gliding away. I let go of Shane and put my face back into the water, looking Mr. Jordan over for any wounds.

"Did he bite him?" Shane shouted.

I couldn't see any signs of injury.

"No," I said. "I think he just bumped him."

"Why do they keep doing that?"

I locked elbows with them again. "Trying to find out what we are," I said.

"What if they come after Dad?"

"I don't know! I don't know, Shane! Do what you can."

Scar rejoined the other two below us for only a moment before breaking away again.

"You watching him?" I said.

"He's gone," Shane replied. "He disappeared. No, I see him. He's on the surface."

I looked to my left and saw Scar's dorsal fin slicing through the top of the water. He seemed to be aiming for Mr. Jordan.

"He's coming at your dad," I said. "Get ready."

19

SCAR VEERED AWAY AN INSTANT BEFORE NOSING MR. JORDAN IN the stomach. He remained out of reach, all eight feet of him passing slowly before my face. I saw his eye up close, staring right at me. Directly below the eye, his mouth gaped in a cruel grin lined with hundreds of knife-edged teeth. The teeth are designed to punch slits so that the shark can pull meat from its prey as easy as tearing a page from a loose-leaf notebook.

Mr. Jordan mumbled something again, and then I felt him struggling. I tried to hold on to his arm, but he managed to twist away.

"Hold your dad, Shane!"

"I've got him!"

"Come on," Mr. Jordan said.

I saw that Shane still had a hold of his other arm, but now our protective triangle was open and I was hanging out at one end of it.

"What's he doing?" I said.

"I don't know. Crap, they're all under us again."

"How many?"

"Three. All three."

I desperately wanted to look down, but I felt more pressed to get us back into formation. At the same time I knew that it was dangerous to splash any more than we had to. I swept my free arm slowly through the water, trying to reach Mr. Jordan again.

"Keep watching them," I said.

Then I saw a glint of steel flash past my wrist. I jerked my arm back and saw Mr. Jordan had his dive knife out, slashing aimlessly through the water with it. I'd narrowly missed getting cut.

"Come on," he murmured again.

"He's got his knife out, Shane!"

"What do you want me to do about it?"

"Get it from him!"

I swung around behind Shane and grabbed hold of his BCD. I watched as he worked his way behind his father and tried reaching over his shoulder for the arm waving the knife.

"Give it to me, Dad!" he said.

Mr. Jordan didn't seem to hear him.

"Give me the knife!"

Mr. Jordan began to struggle, and Shane put his arm around his neck.

"Get away from me," Mr. Jordan growled.

Shane hugged him close until his chin was over his dad's shoulder.

"You gotta stop, Dad!" Shane cried. "You gotta put the knife up!"

But Mr. Jordan only struggled more. He began lifting his arm from the water repeatedly, plunging the knife blade down at his imaginary sharks.

"Get away from me!" Mr. Jordan yelled.

"Stop it, Dad!"

"Let go of him!" I shouted. "The splashing attracts them!"

Shane shook his dad and hit at the side of his face. "Dad, stop!" he cried. "Stop!"

Now both of them were splashing and frantic, and it didn't look like there was any way to reason with Mr. Jordan. And he was only moments from cutting one of us. I jerked at Shane's BCD, trying to pull him off.

"Let go, Shane! Get away from him!"

Then I heard a tearing sound and a hiss. Bubbles began to rise around us. I brought my feet up and kicked against Mr. Jordan's back, trying to pull Shane off him, but it wasn't enough. I smacked Shane's head, trying to get his attention.

"Let him go!"

Shane went limp and it flashed through my mind that maybe he'd been stabbed.

Mr. Jordan started to yell something, but then the yell was cut off as his face slipped beneath the water. I suddenly realized I was dangerously tied to two people I could no longer control. I reached to my ankle and drew my knife and cut the line that was holding us together. Then I stretched around Shane and cut the line between him and his dad. After shoving the knife back in the sheath and regaining my hold on Shane's BCD, I pulled my feet up and kicked out at Mr. Jordan again with everything I had. His head slipped through Shane's elbow and we were suddenly free of him. I grabbed Shane, and swam us backward.

"Grab his line!" I said.

Shane reached out and grabbed the trailing end of Mr. Jordan's line that I'd cut. Both of us watched his dad flail about with the knife, trying to stay afloat in a deflated BCD. I knew with his weights still attached it was impossible. He went under, then appeared again, looking at us this time with wide, crazed eyes.

"I can't hold it!" Shane cried.

"Try," I said, grasping him tightly. "He's going to kill us all. There's nothing else we can do."

I passed one hand quickly over Shane's BCD to make sure it was still inflated. It felt firm.

Mr. Jordan gasped and went under again. I watched Shane's arm stretch out and the line slip through his fist.

I spun him around to face me. His eyes were red and wide, and he was breathing rapidly.

I didn't want to put my dive mask back on. I didn't want to see what was going on below us. I only knew we needed to get out of there.

I jerked the fins out of my BCD and shoved them at Shane.

"Put them on," I said.

Shane stared at me and didn't move.

I held the speargun to my chest with an elbow and clamped one of his fins in my teeth. I went under and grabbed his leg and lifted it and started cramming his foot into the other one. It seemed impossible with everything I was holding. Then I dropped the speargun in my struggle and caught a blurry glimpse of it sinking into the depths.

Panic flooded me. I resurfaced and got a breath.

"Help me!" I yelled.

Shane reached down like he was about to do something, but I didn't have the patience for him. I dove beneath the surface again and managed to get the fin strap around his ankle. Then I grabbed his other foot, shoved on the second fin, and strapped it. I came up, jerked my own fins from his back, and crammed them on.

To my relief, Shane grabbed hold of me and started kicking. Then we were both kicking with everything we had.

20

THE SHARKS WERE GONE. MR. JORDAN WAS GONE. THE BLUE water carried Shane and me along, our legs hanging limp below us, the sun beating down on our sun masks. After we stopped swimming I tied us together again, but nothing I did now seemed of any use.

Neither of us had spoken a word since we'd left his dad. Shane seemed too weak, too much in shock to express his feelings over what had happened, whatever those feelings might be.

Mother Nature's going to finish us off. She's only holding on to us a little longer for her amusement.

My thirst was torturous and my skin crawled and

burned with the thousands of tiny sea lice stinging me. I imagined by now they'd worked their way inside Shane's wetsuit, too. My body seemed nothing more than a lump of soggy, bug-infested meat carrying a brain. And until the bugs got to my brain I'd have to float like this and feel them eat the rest of me away.

The thought of drowning myself always got stuck like a switch inside me that I couldn't flip. It really didn't make sense that killing yourself couldn't be more of an option, especially when you knew with all certainly you were going to die anyway. But I couldn't imagine not seeing Mom and Dad again. And I'd have to take off my wetsuit if I wanted to sink, and I didn't want Shane seeing me naked. I suddenly laughed to myself.

"What?" Shane said through trembling teeth.

"I was thinking that I didn't want you to see me naked."

"Why is that funny?"

"Because it's so stupid. That I would care about something like that now."

"Why are you even talking about it?"

"I was thinking about drowning. It's going to be hard to drown as long as I have a wetsuit on. I'd have to take it off. And then you'd see me naked."

"Whatever," he said. "I'm just cold. I'm so cold and thirsty."

The neoprene of Shane's wetsuit was only 3 millimeters, or mils, thick. I had on a 5 mil, and the extra thickness was keeping me a little warmer. Especially now that we'd stopped swimming, the Gulf water was steadily bringing down our core body temperatures. It was probably close to 85 degrees Fahrenheit, but even that'll kill you if you're exposed to it long enough. When the sun set again we'd get even colder, and eventually both of us were going to become hypothermic.

I got behind Shane and unclipped the front of my BCD so that it spread open. Then I stuck my arms up the front of his BCD and hugged him and felt him shaking against me. I had never been so close to a boy. I had always been nervous about if and when and how I would find myself in such a situation. Now, even though I wished our circumstances were different, I felt relief to get beyond it. And it was more natural and comforting than I'd expected.

"Is that better?" I said over his shoulder.

He nodded. I felt shivers running up his body like electric pulses.

"We're going to have to try to float like this," I said.

Shane stopped shivering not long after I hugged him to me. I managed to wrap my hands inside the straps of his

BCD so I could relax them. Then I rested my chin on his shoulder and somehow I was finally able to drift off to sleep.

I had strange flitting dreams that made no sense. I was at a fancy Cinderella ball and Shane was in a tuxedo. He looked handsome and held my hand, and I was proud to be with him. Then I was standing alone on a beach in a storm. Rain was hitting the calm water like loud static on a television. And this strange noise worked at my ears until I woke and opened my eyes.

It was late afternoon. The sun was setting cool and orange before me and the Gulf water appeared as still as a swimming pool. Then I realized the sound of the rain was still playing in my ears. I lifted my chin from Shane's shoulder. Not a hundred yards from us, in both directions, for what looked like miles, the surface was boiling and popping with small feeding fish.

"Shane?" I said.

He didn't answer.

"Shane?"

"What?" he muttered sleepily.

"You see that?"

"What?"

"The fish."

After a moment he said, "Yes . . . Is that bad?"

"I think it's bluefish or something. They'll probably be scared of us."

"Good."

"You still cold?"

"Yes."

"I know. Me too."

"I think my legs are frozen."

"They're only stiff. Mine are the same way. Try to bend them."

"I am," he said.

I worked one of my legs in front of his ankle and put the other behind his knee and bent it slowly. Then I felt him begin to move it on his own.

"That's better," he said.

I did the same to his other leg.

"Maybe we should swim some," I said. "My legs are feeling stiff, too."

"I don't think I can. I'm too cold."

"Try," I said.

I backed away and fastened my BCD again. I pulled off my sun mask, then pulled Shane's off, too, and stuffed them into my BCD pocket. Then I started kicking slowly and pulling Shane with me. After a moment he was kicking both his legs, and we put our dive masks on our faces and peered down at the endless blue below.

The popping and splashing of the feeding fish grew louder until we began to see the outside edges of the bait, suspended like millions of bits of glass that jerked and flashed about in giant glittering clouds as far as we could see into the depths. Bluefish and jack crevalle raced through, the clouds dispersing then re-forming. Then the feeding frenzy parted and closed in behind us and continued on all sides like we were nothing more than a small blister on the surface of it. And for a moment I was mesmerized, forgetting about my thirst and the cold water and the sea lice and thinking it was the most beautiful thing I'd ever seen. And thinking that if I were to die and slowly sink to the bottom that it wouldn't be such a bad way to go.

21

WHEN WE STOPPED SWIMMING THERE WAS ONLY A SLIVER OF sun left on the horizon. The wide expanse of feeding fish had broken up and existed only in patches like isolated rain hitting the water. I unclipped and hugged Shane to me and pressed my cheek to his cold face. In that way we watched the last of the sun sinking into the water like a dying coal.

The night sky was moonless, but the stars were thick and cast a soft glow over the calm water. Below our feet jellyfish hovered like green and pink night lights.

How can Mother Nature be so beautiful and so mean at the same time? I thought.

I told myself that if I ignored thoughts of hypothermia my shivering would stop. But then all I could think about was my thirst and the bugs and the possibility of dying, which brought me back to being cold and miserable again.

"I think I'm going to die tonight," Shane said.

"No you're not," I said.

"What's the point in this?"

"If we go, we go together."

"I don't know if I can wait."

"Don't stop talking to me," I said.

"I'm so tired of it all," he said.

"I don't think you should sleep."

"Do you think the sharks ate him?"

"We can talk about anything but that."

"Why didn't they come after us?"

"I don't know. They lost interest."

"I don't want to go like that."

"You won't. He went crazy."

"You can't let that happen to me, no matter what."

"It won't happen to you. I'm going to stay with you."

"He never touched me, you know."

I didn't answer. I didn't understand.

"I mean, he shook my hand sometimes, like I was a grown-up or something. But he never patted me on the back or put his arm around me."

"I'm sorry," I said.

"Sometimes I wished he were dead. And I'm wondering now if I got my wish and I'm being punished for it."

"But you didn't really wish that."

"I did," Shane said. "But it wasn't like I thought it would really happen. You know, it's like a bully at school that you don't want to deal with."

"Yeah," I said. "I get it."

Shane was quiet for a few minutes.

"Shane?" I said.

"What?"

"I'm going to keep talking to you. Every few minutes. To make sure you don't go to sleep."

"Okay," he said.

"I think if you go to sleep you'll die."

"Okay," he said.

Now it seemed there was no difference between me and Shane. He was a boy and I was a girl, but mostly we'd been reduced to two people simply staying alive. And right there, at that moment, he was the most important person in the world to me. I couldn't think of anything worse than losing him and being alone. And just the day before I'd hated him with all my heart.

22

THE JORDANS HAD BEEN THIRTY MINUTES LATE FOR THEIR charter. Dad and I heard them arguing outside the dive shop before they came through the door. Then Shane entered in a huff, his dive bag slung over his shoulder.

"Use the old one," Mr. Jordan was saying to him. "Chill out about it, will you?"

"I liked my new one," Shane snapped.

"What do you want me to do about it?"

"I want you to put it in my dive bag next time."

Mr. Jordan dropped his equipment on the floor beside his son's. Shane looked at Dad and then me like he realized for the first time we were also in the room. I was sure he recognized me, but he didn't act like it.

Mr. Jordan approached Dad. "How's the visibility out there?"

"Should be pretty good," Dad said. "It was good a couple of days ago. But you never know until you get in the water."

"You got anything decent we can dive?"

Dad smiled smugly. "Yeah, I've got something decent."

"What? Like that old Lipscomb tug you took me to last year?"

"I suppose that's where all the other outfits would take you."

"You're right, Gib," he said. "There's three other dive shops I could've gone to today. The only reason I'm standing here right now is because they're booked up. And unless you've got something to offer me that they don't, I doubt I'll be back."

Dad maintained his sly grin for a moment longer, then said, "Well, you came to the right place, Hank. How do a couple of untouched army tanks sound? Three years down. Never been fished or dove."

Mr. Jordan raised his eyebrows with interest. "Where?"

"About thirty miles out."

"Whose are they?"

"Mine. I put them out there."

Mr. Jordan studied him suspiciously. "How'd you pull that off?"

"Don't worry about it."

Mr. Jordan smiled and nodded slowly. "I see," he said. "Your big secret spot. Well, you got my attention. So what's this going to cost me?"

"Two thousand. One dive."

I looked at Dad. He'd never charged that much. I looked at Mr. Jordan. He hadn't flinched at the price. He actually appeared to be considering it.

"What about two dives?" Shane interjected.

Dad kept his eyes on Mr. Jordan. "One dive," Dad said. "Then we head in."

Mr. Jordan didn't respond. I could see he didn't like someone being firm with him.

"Or," Dad continued, "for your standard four hundred and fuel we can drop anchor at one of those fished-out public reefs like everyone else. Your choice."

"What's the depth?" Mr. Jordan asked.

"Hundred and five feet," Dad said.

Mr. Jordan reached into his bag and pulled out his dive chart and studied it. "That's twenty minutes of bottom time without decompression." He looked up. "That's a hundred dollars a minute."

Dad shrugged with a take-it-or-leave-it look.

Mr. Jordan dropped the chart back into his bag and looked at his son. "You want to do it?"

Shane nodded greedily.

Mr. Jordan turned back to Dad. I saw his weasel brain working.

"I'll give you five thousand dollars for the coordinates."

I looked at Dad. That kind of money could solve a lot of our problems. Minutes before, I would have told him to take it. But if it was really this easy to get two thousand per trip, we'd make even more than that in a week.

"No deal," Dad said. "My only offer's on the table."

Mr. Jordan stared at him, and I could imagine him using that same look to scare people in the courtroom. For the first time in a long while I felt myself swelling with pride for Dad. I couldn't remember the last time I'd seen him stand up to someone with such confidence.

"Fine," Mr. Jordan finally said. "We'll do it. Remind me how this works. Pay now or later?"

"You can—"

"You pay us now," I interrupted.

Mr. Jordan looked at me.

Dad smiled. "That's my daughter, Julie," he said. "I suppose she's the boss when it comes to the money."

I could tell Mr. Jordan didn't like the idea of me getting into the middle of things. He turned to Dad again and pulled out his wallet. As he thumbed a stack of cash onto the counter I brought him a pen and a waiver form. He glanced over the paper and signed it. I picked it up with the money and counted the bills. When I saw that it was the right amount I looked at Dad and nodded.

Dad slapped his palms on the counter. "All right," he said. "Let's get you boys out there."

I thought I would have felt better holding that money, but I didn't. It all seemed too rushed and thrown together from the beginning.

23

"JULIE?" SHANE SAID.

"What?"

"I see a light."

"A light?"

"Yeah," he said, like he'd already studied it for a while.

I thought he was imagining things. I put my face against his cheek again and tried to line my eyes up with whatever he was looking at.

"It's red and flashing," he said.

I didn't see anything at first. Then I picked out a soft red glow just above the horizon.

I was flooded with hope as I considered that red light had to be connected to civilization in some way. Then I reasoned that no land would be this close to blue water. And a boat would have more lights and would never see us even if we could swim to it fast enough.

"It's probably a plane," I said.

"A plane would have other lights, too," Shane said.

I thought about that and decided he was right. Planes showed red and green and white like a boat.

I kicked my fins and raised my head a few more inches above his shoulder and saw the light glow again.

"How far away do you think it is?" Shane asked.

"I don't know," I said. "It's hard to tell."

The light blinked again.

"If it's moving," I continued, "it's not moving very fast."

"I can't swim that far," he said.

"It seems like we're moving toward it . . . Hold on."

I let loose of Shane and got out my compass, which still glowed enough for me to read it. I got a bearing on the light and saw that it was south-southeast of us. Then I pulled out the marker and dropped it. I watched the line unspool until the end of it was yanked from my fingers and for a moment I watched the cork trail past the jellyfish into the depths.

"It's too deep," I said.

"Too deep for what?"

Shane hadn't noticed that I'd lost the marker. It didn't seem to matter.

"We're probably still drifting to the southeast. So we need to alter our course to the southwest to intercept it."

Shane didn't answer.

"We need to swim crosscurrent," I said. "We might be able to make it."

"My legs are so numb I don't think I can get them working again."

"We have to try," I said.

I dove under and grabbed one of his legs, bent it, and straightened it. Then I did the same to the other and re-surfaced.

"Anything?" I asked.

"A little," he said.

Suddenly I couldn't stand the thought of us losing more valuable time. I grabbed his arm and began to kick. "I think I can pull us awhile," I said. "Keep trying."

I put on my dive mask, kept my face down, and paddled us silently along. When I wasn't catching a breath or glancing at my compass I stared past the jellyfish into the endless dark. I imagined moving above the corduroy ripples of the seafloor hundreds of feet below, and this thought gave me a sense of progress. After a while I stopped and got another compass heading on the light. It seemed like we hadn't moved at all. I felt panic begin to grip me.

"You've got to kick, Shane," I said. "I can't do this alone."

"I've been trying," he said.

"You've got to try harder! We can't make it like this!"

24

I SAW THAT SHANE WASN'T GOING TO BE ABLE TO GET MOVING on his own. I got in front of him, went under, and lifted his legs until he was floating on his back.

"Grab them with your arms," I said. "Try to pull your knees to your chest."

He began to move his arms slowly toward his knees. I grabbed his hand and helped him. I watched him clutch the neoprene of his wetsuit at the knees. He tugged at it until the rubbery material popped loose. I became frustrated. I put one arm behind his neck and one behind his knee, cradling him like a baby, and folded his left leg up to his chest.

"Now straighten it," I said.

He slowly straightened the leg and a wave of hope passed through me. I swam around to his other side, did the same thing, then let him bob upright again.

"Try now," I said.

I put my face into the water and watched his legs as he was able to slowly bend and straighten them. Afraid of losing more time, I grabbed his arm and began pulling him.

"Keep working them," I said.

Gradually Shane was able to start kicking enough to take away some of my burden. But the red light still appeared an impossible distance away, and I began to doubt that we'd actually make it. Current direction changes all the time, and I was basing our heading on information that was over a day old. But at least trying got us both moving again and warmed us up.

After nearly an hour of steady swimming I was exhausted. I got a final compass bearing and saw that it was now mostly southeast of us. And until we narrowed the distance some, and really saw how we were drifting, there was no sense in wasting more strength.

"You okay?" I said.

"My teeth are chattering again," he said, "but at least I can swim a little. That thing doesn't seem any closer."

"I think it is," I said. "It certainly isn't any farther away, which is good."

"What if it's land? What if it's an island?"

"I don't know how it *could* be," I said. "There's no way. So don't get your hopes up."

"How can I not get my hopes up? It's probably the last chance we've got. We're dying, Julie. If that light doesn't help us, we're finished."

"Let's rest and save our energy," I said. "We're going to have to swim some more when we get closer."

"You may have to work my legs again," he said.

"Okay," I said. I didn't want to tell him, but now my legs and arms were getting stiff, too. If we were going to make it at all, we needed to make it fast.

For two more hours we paddled steadily while the red light appeared to rise very slowly above the horizon. Gradually I discerned a patch of darkness beneath it. We were probably a mile away when I knew what it was.

"An oil rig," I said.

Shane didn't respond.

I felt myself become overwhelmed with hope.

"Shane, I think it's a floating oil rig!"

"I'll bet they have ski jackets," he mumbled.

"What are you talking about?"

"And beach towels."

I realized he was delirious, in the advanced stages of hypothermia. I grabbed my compass and got a reading.

"It's a little bit more to the west," I said. "We need to swim harder. Can you do it?"

"Sure, I can do it. I'm on the cross-country team."

I cradled him and tried to force his knees to his chest, but his muscles were much stiffer this time. I couldn't even get him into a sitting position.

"Ugh," I groaned, frustrated. I grabbed his knee and shoved it hard, but it only pushed him away from me until he came tight against the line. I watched him bob upright again.

"Let's call a taxi," he said.

It was all I could do to stay calm. I pulled him to me again and began rubbing his legs, but my arms were stiff, too, and I couldn't apply much pressure.

"Get my cell phone," he said.

"There's no taxis or phones," I said. "You have to swim, Shane! You have to try!"

"It's in my pocket."

I started shaking and coughing. As dehydrated as I was, it was as close as my body could come to crying. I grabbed him by the straps of his BCD and shook him. "We came too far for this, Shane!"

He stared back at me quizzically. I thought about the consequences of leaving him, and I was forced to consider something about the rig that had been bothering me. There should have been more than one red light on it. It should have been lit like an amusement park if there were people working and living on it.

"What if there's nobody on that thing?" I said. "I can't send anybody for you!"

"It's okay," he said.

"No, it's *not* okay."

I turned him on his back, grabbed his arm, and began kicking, dragging him like a log. My legs were so stiff and numb that it seemed like my fins barely moved. I didn't know if it was possible to make it, but I knew I couldn't live with myself if I left him.

It rose before us like an abandoned steel city supported nearly a hundred feet above the surface by four enormous floating columns and a crosswork of beams connecting them. As I struggled to pull us closer I began to hear water licking and slurping through the massive beams of its understructure. Otherwise, there was no sound coming from it at all. Only the soft red glow of the hazard light from the top of the derrick.

My body was about to shut down. I had to force every

kick, all the while fearing I couldn't make it. We were going to pass within a hundred yards, but that hundred yards might as well have been a mile. It wasn't possible.

"I can't do it, Shane," I sputtered. "I can't make it."

But Shane wasn't answering. He hadn't said a word since I'd started dragging him. Part of me wanted to stop and check on him to see if he was still breathing, but I reasoned that it didn't matter now. And I really didn't want to know.

I stopped swimming and let go of Shane and floated there, staring at the black wall towering over us. I had never felt such helplessness. I could only watch myself drift from the last chance of ever seeing my parents again. Continuing on into complete darkness. A final goodbye to life.

25

I FELT SOMETHING TAP MY SIDE. I IMMEDIATELY THOUGHT OF sharks and spun and kicked. In the faint light of the sky glow I saw a long seam in the water next to me. I reached out and touched a rope as big around as my arm. I grabbed it and felt it move heavily atop the surface.

A mooring line.

"Shane!"

I shook him.

"Shane! I've got a rope!"

He muttered something I didn't understand. I began pulling myself along the rope, towing Shane behind me. Slowly I drew us into the dark night-shadow of the rig.

When we were about fifty yards away the rope began to curve up into the air to a lower platform about twenty feet overhead. I was facing a crosscurrent swim to make it the rest of the distance to the understructure, where I hoped to find something to climb onto. There was no way I could do it towing Shane with me.

"Listen, Shane," I said. "Can you hear me?"

He didn't answer.

"I'm going to have to tie you off to this rope while I try to get up there. Then I'll figure out a way to get you up. Okay?"

No answer.

I untied the line from my BCD and tied it to the mooring rope. This time I doubled the strength of the line for safe measure.

"I'll be back, okay? Float here until I figure it out."

I kicked toward the understructure. Fortunately there were no tall waves. In rough seas there would be no way to approach the steel beams without getting slammed and cut to pieces on the millions of barnacles cemented to every part of the lower structure. I could already hear the beams clicking and snapping as the Gulf swells rose and fell over them.

I pulled both of our sun masks out of my BCD pocket. The swells were gentle enough that I figured if I protected my hands from the barnacles, I might be able to hold on to something. I stuck my fists inside the cloth and tucked the edges into the wrists of my wetsuit.

As I drew nearer, the swells lifted and dropped me before a massive grid of iron that slurped and glistened in the shadows. On the next uplift I reached out and touched the steel and let my hands slide lightly down the barnacles before drifting away again. On the next approach I moved over a few feet, rose up, and ran my hands over the steel again. This time I felt a ledge that I could hold on to. I gripped it, feeling the barnacles press sharply into my makeshift gloves.

When the swell dropped I was left hanging there, barely able to hold on. The weight was too much for my gloves, and I clenched my jaw in pain as the barnacles pressed through the cloth and cut into the soggy skin of my palms like glass shards. Then I realized there was no way to climb with my fins on. I waited until the next swell supported me, then let go with one hand to work my fins off with the other. The barnacles cut deeper into my palm and the pain was excruciating.

I tore the fins off, let them fall into the water, then grabbed the steel with both hands again. Scraping my feet around, I quickly found a foothold below me. My booties protected my feet from being cut, and I had to keep as much weight on them as I could. Once I was supporting my weight, I grabbed higher and pulled myself up with what felt like the last of my strength. And finally I was out of the cold water for the first time in nearly forty-eight hours. But I was exhausted and clinging to a thin lip of steel with shredded hands and trembling knees. I couldn't hang on for long, and I was certain I didn't have the strength to do it again.

To my left I saw a steel beam angling up toward one of the columns where it was welded to what appeared to be a low platform about four feet wide. I reached out, grabbed the beam, and fell over onto it, feeling more barnacles cut into my hands and through the legs of my wetsuit. I crawled up the beam, out of the barnacle zone, and under a railing. I rolled across the steel grate of the platform and I was suddenly lying on my back and free of the cruel salt water.

As I lay resting, the waves rose and fell beneath me like snapping dogs. I began to study the underside of the rig and saw more of the small platforms ascending the outside of the column and connected with ladder rungs. I wanted more than anything to lie there and rest, but I thought of Shane drifting alone and I forced myself to get up again. I left the cloth on my hands to offer what little protection it could for the deep slices on my palms.

Then I started up the ladder into the bowels of this mysteriously abandoned superstructure.

The underside of the rig was enormous. As I climbed higher, sky glow reflecting off the water illuminated the steel in pale hues of wavering light. I must have ascended a hundred ladder steps, my footfalls echoing dull and loud under the lonely place. My hands felt sticky and oily with blood and I told myself it was a good thing I couldn't see them, since it would only worry me more. They were going to have to work for me no matter how they felt and what shape they were in.

At the last of the platforms beneath the rig I found myself looking down at the Gulf swells a hundred feet below. Overhead was a confusing network of pipes and metal catwalks crisscrossing in the faint light. One of the catwalks led to a staircase that descended to the mooring dock where Shane's rope was tied. I still didn't have any idea how I was going to get him up, but I decided to start off by inspecting the area and seeing what all I had to work with.

I made my way over and down to the dock, where I found the rope fastened to a giant cleat. I looked over the water and saw a dark lump against the rope that I assumed was Shane. The way it was drifting perpendicular to the current told me it must be tied off or hung on something beyond the rig. There appeared to be enough slack in it to pull Shane to me, but even if I'd had all my strength and my hands weren't cut, the rope itself was too heavy to lift twenty feet, much less with Shane on it. Then another crushing thought came over me.

What if the line tying him to the rope didn't hold?

I remembered that I'd doubled the strength of it, but in his condition Shane wasn't going to be any help, and all of his weight would rely on only two strands of that thin line.

But I didn't see any other options. I had to somehow try to pull him up and hope the line held.

26

EXCEPT FOR SOME SHORT PIECES OF SUN-BLEACHED LINE, THE dock was empty of anything I could use to reach Shane. Then I saw a thinner rope and a cable dangling from above. I looked up to see the cable attached to a crane near the top of the rig. The rope had a hook on the end and seemed to lead to what looked like a smaller winch. I started up the stairs again until I was standing on the first level of the rig. Judging by the rope spools and barrels and other equipment, I guessed the space was some sort of staging area for supplies. There was even a gate in the railing designed to swing open and accept materials transferred from below. I examined the winch and saw that it was electric, but it also had a manual crank that operated much like the ones we had on boat trailers. I flipped the cog lock on it and began spooling off-line. When the hook at the end was below the mooring dock I relocked the cog and hurried back down.

On the dock again, I grabbed the winch hook and fastened it around Shane's mooring rope. Then I untied the mooring rope from the cleat.

"Hold on if you can, Shane!" I shouted below. "I'm going to try to pull you up!"

I hurried back up to the winch and began cranking the handle by pressing against it with the undersides of my wrists. Eighty feet below, the mooring rope arced out and I saw the dark speck at the end of it slowly moving toward the rig. I tried to recall exactly where I'd tied the line to him. I didn't want him getting pulled up by an arm or, even worse, his neck.

His BCD. It's tied to the straps of his BCD. That's good. As good as it can be.

I kept cranking. The angle of the mooring rope straightened. I could no longer see Shane, but I knew by the angle and the tension that he was about to be lifted from the water. I pinched the winch rope with an outstretched arm and counted the clicks of the cog. Three clicks reeled about a foot of rope.

Three clicks per foot. Twenty feet. Three times twenty is sixty, less the three clicks I just did. So . . . fifty-seven.

I began cranking again and counting cog clicks. When I got to fifty I saw Shane below, dangling by his BCD. I hurried off seven more clicks and dashed back down to the dock.

When I arrived I found him swinging outside and above the railing. I grabbed one of the short pieces of line lying on the grate, climbed onto the railing, and tied it to the winch rope over his head. Then I climbed down again and pulled on the line until he swung over the dock. I tied it off to leave him suspended before me at eye level. I was so happy I felt like crying.

"Hey, there," I said.

"Hey," he muttered.

I was reminded that he was in no condition to celebrate or even know what was happening.

"Hold on," I said. "This might hurt."

I pulled my dive knife, got under him, and cut the winch rope from his waist. Shane came falling on top of me, and both of us went down to the deck in a heap.

I lay there for a moment, allowing myself a small rest while my hands throbbed in pain. But it wasn't long before I knew I needed to keep moving. We needed water and warmth while I still had the strength to get it for us.

The first thing I had to do was stabilize Shane. Concerned that he might roll overboard in his delirium, I re-tied the line on his BCD to the steel grate so that he could move only a foot in either direction. Then I stood to go.

"I'll be back," I told him.

I returned to the staging area near the winch and looked over the piles of equipment. Seeing nothing I could use, I tried the knob on a steel door to my left. The knob turned, and the door swung inward on creaky hinges, releasing a breath of hot musty air. I only stared into the dark interior for a moment before I realized it was useless trying to find anything in there without a light. Then I backed away and looked farther along the outside of the rig. Down from me were two lifeboats. They were the enclosed models, bulbous pods with windows down the side and a hatch on the top. I knew they usually carried survival supplies.

27

I MADE MY WAY TO THE FIRST BOAT AND AFTER A FEW MINUTES,
with limited use of my hands, I was able to figure out
how to get the entry door open. I dropped inside and
there was just enough light coming through the hatch
and windows to see rows of benches and a tiny control
room forward to drive and steer the vessel. It looked like
it would hold about twenty people. In the aisle between
the benches was a long storage box. I lifted the lid and
searched inside. It was too dark to see everything, but
one by one I felt things and lifted them up to the light
and examined them. It wasn't long before I'd collected a
pack of emergency thermal blankets, six bottled waters,

and a first aid kit. I shoved these items out of the hatch and climbed up after them.

Back on the deck, I opened one of the waters and took a small swallow and felt the liquid soak into my tongue and roll down my throat like rivulets through a desert. I took another swallow and savored it for a moment before reminding myself that Shane was waiting. I gathered two more bottles and the blankets, then hurried back to the stairs.

I untied Shane from the mooring line and sat him up. I took his mask from around his neck and poured water into his mouth, most of it running down the side of his face. Then he tasted it, and I poured again and he swallowed. I removed his BCD and—through much effort and pain— tugged off his fins, booties, wetsuit, and skinsuit until he was wearing nothing but his swim trunks. After a short rest I spread his wetsuit behind him like a mat, rolled him onto it, and shoved the BCD under his head for a pillow. I tore open the pack of emergency blankets and found six of them inside. They looked like nothing more than thin reflective plastic, but I knew they would help preserve Shane's body heat. I pulled him up again and got one of the blankets behind him and let him back down. Finally I wrapped him and put another one over the top and tucked the edges under the wetsuit mat.

"That'll help until the sun comes up," I said. "Here's more water."

I poured another swallow into his mouth. He tasted it and gulped and brought his hands up to clutch the bottle. I let him have it and watched for a moment as he shivered and took a drink and breathed and took another drink.

"I'm going back up," I said. "To find more supplies. You okay?"

He lowered the bottle and nodded.

I started up the stairs again, slowly this time, finally able to relax and focus on myself. I drank more of my water, feeling the inside of me slowly coming back to life while the outside of me still shivered and throbbed and burned from the sea lice and saltwater cuts.

I need to clean the cuts. I need to get warm. I need to drink more water.

Back near the lifeboats I sat on the steel floor with the first aid kit. I began peeling the bloody rags from my hands. Some of the cloth tears were punched into the cuts and pasted with blood into the open wounds. When they popped free the pain made me gasp and stop and take deep breaths. When I was done, my hands were dripping with blood, but I managed to tear open a package of gauze and used it to stanch the bleeding. After a couple of minutes I let go of the gauze and pulled off my booties and struggled out of my wetsuit until I was completely naked. Then I pushed myself up and got a bottle of alcohol from the first aid kit.

I opened the bottle and poured it on my legs. I clenched my teeth and gasped as the chemical worked into the wounds like liquid fire. Once the pain subsided I took a few deep breaths and steeled myself for the worst of it. I put the bottle under my chin and tilted it over both my hands at once. The pain was almost more than I could take. I dropped the bottle and screamed and lay back with my hands out at my sides. It felt like I was holding my fists in pots of boiling water. Teetering on the verge of blacking out, I stayed paralyzed, taking deep breaths, and waiting for the agony to end.

After a few minutes the alcohol had done its work. I forced myself up again and tore open several bandages, pressed them over the wounds, and wrapped them with more gauze. I was racing against my body, trying to patch it up before I passed out. Finally, I rolled over and grabbed another one of the survival blankets, ripped it open with my teeth, and gathered it around me. Then I balled up like a baby and sobbed.

28

I OPENED MY EYES TO STARE OUT OVER THE BLUE EXPANSE OF THE
Gulf. The sun was just above the horizon. It was strange
not to hear the cries of seagulls feeding in the dawn light,
but I knew we were too far from land to see birds. All I
heard was the slurping of the swells rising and falling
through the understructure of the rig, the breeze whistling around the steel, and thunder rumbling in the distance.

I rolled out of the blanket and onto my back to feel
the breeze over my naked body. It felt so good to be dry
again. The air over my skin killed the sea lice and brought
instant relief to the sores and sunburn. I lay there for a

moment, thankful for every second I wasn't back in the cold grips of the Gulf water below. But it was only a moment before I felt my legs and palms throbbing again.

I brought my hands before my face and studied them. The rough bandaging job I'd done had held, but the gauze was already bloody and needed changing. I crawled on my forearms to the railing and looked down. Shane had rolled onto his side and appeared to be sleeping. I backed away, got to my feet, and clutched the emergency blanket about myself. I sensed there was no one but the two of us for a hundred miles, but I still couldn't bring myself to stand completely exposed on a high platform.

I looked around. All about me was the massive rig in its state of eerie abandonment. The door I'd peered into earlier was still open, and I approached it and looked inside. In the faint light I saw shelves of valves and rubber hoses and racks of iron pipe. Boxes of nuts and bolts and other spare parts. To my left was a long counter with wrenches, screwdrivers, and other tools scattered across it like someone had been working there and hurried away before cleaning up.

I flipped a light switch and nothing happened. I opened the door wider and saw a stack of shelves to my right. On one shelf was a box that read JUMPSUITS and another not far from it that said SAFETY GLASSES and HARD HATS and GLOVES. The gloves would enable me to better use my hands while they healed, and the jumpsuit was something to cover up with. I grabbed two pairs of gloves and the two smallest jumpsuits I could find and left the room.

I sat down beside the lifeboats and got into my new outfit. It was a little big, but once I tucked the pant legs into my booties it worked fine. Then I pulled on the gloves, happy they were big enough to fit over my bandaged hands. Finally I grabbed the other jumpsuit, along with two more bottles of water I'd pulled from the lifeboat, and left to check on Shane.

As I descended the stairs I saw him roll over and look up at me. His face was like cracked shoe leather, while his skin from the neck down was fish-meat white and dotted with hundreds of red sores. As bad as he appeared, I knew I probably looked worse.

"Why are you dressed like that?" he said.

I sat down beside him.

"I'll tell you later," I said. "Drink some more water."

"How'd we get up here?" he said.

"I pulled you up," I said, "with a winch."

I helped him sit, and we both opened the bottles and began drinking.

"Where is everybody?" he asked.

"I think we're it," I said. "I think it's abandoned."

"How can this thing be abandoned?"

"I don't know, but I haven't heard any engines running

155

and I haven't seen anyone. I did find a storage room full of equipment. It wasn't even locked."

"Equipment like that jumpsuit?"

"Yeah. And I brought one for you, too."

"What's with the gloves?"

"I hurt my hands. They're fine."

After we'd each finished our water I unfolded the jumpsuit and passed it to him. "Try it on," I said. "There's more if it doesn't fit."

"I'm fine like I am," he replied. "It feels good being out of that wetsuit."

"Well, you better put on your booties if you want to walk on these steel grates."

After Shane pulled on his booties I helped him stand. He steadied himself against the railing and looked down at the swells below.

"Think you can walk upstairs?" I asked him.

"Yeah, but I might need some help. My legs are kind of shaky."

I helped him up the stairs, and by the time we were at the top he was mostly walking on his own. I led him over near the lifeboats.

"I got the water and stuff out of one of those boats last night," I said. "There's more survival gear in there if we need it."

"Food?"

"Probably. Let's sit here and rest for a few minutes," I said. "And drink some more water. We need to hydrate."

"Sure," he said.

"Then we'll go exploring and see what we can find."

29

WE LAY IN THE SHADE OUTSIDE THE STORAGE ROOM, RESTING and drinking water. After a while Shane said he was feeling better and he wanted to check out the lifeboats.

I waited while he climbed into the first one. I heard him bumping around inside for a few minutes before he poked his head out of the hatch.

"It's got like a throttle and steering wheel and everything, but nothing works. The batteries must be dead."

"Did you see more bottled water?"

"Yeah. Like three or four cases."

"Good. Look for an EPIRB."

"What's that?"

"Like a satellite signaling device. It's about the size of a handheld radio."

Shane ducked into the boat again. He reappeared a moment later and held up an EPIRB for me to see.

"Like this?" he said.

I felt my spirits soar. "Yes!" I said. "That's it!"

Shane shook his head. "Battery's dead," he said.

"What's the date on it? It should have an expiration date."

Shane studied it. "Says 2014."

I sighed. "That's three years ago. Yeah, it's dead. Check the other boat."

Shane crawled into the second lifeboat. It wasn't long before he reappeared, shaking his head. "Expired," he said.

"See if there's a flashlight that works," I said, "and get the rest of the water."

Shane found a battery-powered lantern that still held a charge. He passed it to me, along with a few more bottles of water.

"There's some chocolate bars and blocks of energy food," he said. "And some flares. There's a bunch more survival stuff we can use."

I waited for Shane to climb down from the lifeboat.

"Let's go look inside," I said.

"How about the other lantern out of that first life-boat?"

I really didn't want to have to carry anything with my hands like they were. "No," I said. "Let's save it. I'll just follow you."

Shane turned on the light and we entered the storage room.

"Smells like a wet dog in here," he said.

"I guess it's been shut up for a while."

He passed the light across the floor and on the shelves. "This is crazy," he said. "There must be thousands of dollars' worth of stuff in here."

At the back of the room was a door.

"Let's see what's through there," Shane said. He pulled the door to him and passed the light over a hall. "I hope there's no dead people in here."

"Shut up," I said.

"Reminds me of zombie movies."

"If you want me to come with you, then stop talking about dead people and zombies."

"I love scary movies," he said.

"You like watching them, not being in them."

We moved slowly down the hall. It was even more hot and musty than the storage room. We came to an open door on our left and I watched as Shane moved the light over its interior.

"Like an office or something," he said. "Look, there's still a computer on the desk."

I peered over his shoulder and saw a desk with a computer monitor and keyboard surrounded by papers and a few fallen ceiling tiles.

"What's the date on the papers?" I asked.

Shane looked at them. "2012," he said.

"Surely this rig hasn't been abandoned for five years."

Shane didn't answer me. He tried the computer's power button, but nothing happened. He shone his light up where the tiles were missing. Others sagged in their tracks, brown and water-stained.

"Let's keep going," I said.

"This must be the work floor," he said. "How many levels are there?"

"It looked like three from the outside."

Shane continued down the hall. "The stairs should be around here somewhere," he said.

We passed three more doors, and Shane paused briefly to inspect the rooms. They were all similar to the first, offices that looked like they'd been left in the middle of a workday. Then we came to a stairwell on our left and the hall continued on in darkness ahead.

"Upstairs?" Shane asked me.

"Yeah," I said. "Upstairs."

30

I GOT BEHIND SHANE AND FOLLOWED AS HE STARTED UP THE stairs. The treads were carpeted and our footfalls landed soft and quiet. When we arrived in another hallway I could no longer hear the sound of the water through the understructure. It was so quiet that my ears hummed. Shane turned right and aimed the light into the first doorway.

"Looks like a lounge," he said.

There were two sofas, a coffee table with magazines scattered over it, and a big-screen television. A bookcase full of paperback books was against the far wall. On the opposite wall was a refrigerator, a sink, and a countertop with shelves over it. Shane stepped through the doorway and approached one of the coffee tables. He picked up a copy of *Sports Illustrated* and studied it.

"Five years old," he said.

"Check the refrigerator," I said.

He walked over to the refrigerator and opened it and an awful stench fell over us.

Shane coughed and backed away. "Holy crap!" he exclaimed.

"What is it?"

Shane shined his light inside. "Oh my God," he said. "It's just one piece of bologna. And it's got so much stuff growing on it that it's like a fungus pizza."

"Ugh," I said.

"How can just one piece of forgotten bologna do that?"

"Close it," I said. "Come on."

Shane coughed again and shut the refrigerator door.

The next room we came to was the galley. It was more like a small cafeteria, looking like it could feed a hundred people. There were about ten tables, all of them with napkin dispensers, and salt and pepper shakers still on them. The air was so thick in the room that the lantern seemed to have a hard time cutting through it.

"Let's check for food," I said.

But Shane was already crossing the floor to a long

stainless-steel countertop. We went around the counter
and through two swinging doors into the kitchen. Pots
and pans and cooking utensils hung from the walls and
ceiling. The stove and countertops were clean except for
bits of fallen ceiling tile. I approached a sink and turned
the faucet. Nothing.

Shane turned the gas knob for the stove. Nothing.

"I doubt anything works," he said.

Shane opened a drawer full of forks, spoons, knives,
and other utensils. "Plenty of silverware," he said. "Can
opener and all kinds of stuff."

"They should have a pantry," I said. "Maybe we'll find
some canned food."

"How long does canned food keep?" he asked.

"I don't know," I said.

Shane shone the light around until we saw a door at
the rear of the kitchen. We entered into another room
equally as large. Along one wall were shelves of scattered
cooking supplies: industrial-size cans of shortening, gal-
lon jugs of vegetable oil, and spices. Then Shane turned
the light on the other wall and we saw more shelves with
a few cans of fruits and vegetables. Next to that were
more cans, of tuna fish and other meats.

"It's something," he said.

"Yeah," I said.

Shane shone the light at the back of the room, where we saw a freezer door.

"No sense checking that," he said. "Probably a giant piece of bologna in there."

I smiled at his joke. "Shine back on the cans," I said. "We can take something with us."

I put a can opener in my pocket and got a large can of peaches and put it under my arm. Shane started back the way we'd come. "There's got to be like some kind of emergency phone on here," he said. "Or a control room with communications equipment."

I followed him back to the stairs, where we ascended to what I assumed was the top level of the rig. Then he turned left down another hall. It seemed like the deeper we traveled into the rig, the more stale and thick the air became. I was starting to feel a little queasy breathing it.

"I think we're somewhere in the middle of this thing," Shane said. "We need to get to the edges to find an outside door or a window."

"Some fresh air," I said.

"Yeah," he said. "This place is rank."

We continued down the hall, passing more doors and not even stopping to look inside. We came to another staircase, and Shane turned toward it and started up. I saw sunlight falling across the floor as we neared the top of the stairwell. We entered a small room with windows and an exit leading outside. Beyond was a helicopter pad.

"Let's get some air," Shane said.

"Gladly," I said.

31

WE STOOD IN THE CENTER OF THE HELICOPTER PAD, FEELING THE wind on our faces and looking across the blue water over a hundred feet below. The swells appeared like small, harmless ripples. Standing at such heights without a railing made me nervous, but the thrill of it outweighed the fright. And it was a relief to have such open space about me after experiencing the creepy interior of the oil rig.

A line of dark thunderclouds was closing in on us from the west, and we watched the heat lightning flicker deep within. The red light we'd seen while we were afloat glowed steadily atop the drilling derrick, nearly a hundred feet overhead.

"Let's rest here," Shane said. "I'm a little light-headed."

We both sat, and I slid the peaches and the can opener to him. "Feel like eating some peaches?"

"Sure," he said.

Shane opened the can and we immediately smelled something like rancid cheese.

"Don't think so," he said.

I frowned and shook my head. "Yeah, definitely bad. I hope all that stuff's not bad."

"I'm sure we can find *something* to eat," Shane said. "After we rest we'll keep searching the top floor."

"We can always catch fish if we have to. I still don't feel much like eating, but we have to get some food in us."

"And we need to find a place to sleep," Shane said.

"I can't stay in there unless we can open some windows," I said. "I'd rather sleep outside."

After a short rest we left the helicopter pad, went inside, and took the stairs back down to the hall that ran along the third level of the rig. The first door we came to opened into a conference room with a large table that must have seated twenty people. There was a speaker phone in the center. Shane picked up the phone, listened, shook his head, and set it down again. I pointed to some cabinets and he held the lantern on them while I looked inside. I found an unopened can of cashews and showed them to him.

"It's something," he said. "I doubt nuts can get that bad."

"Yeah," I said, passing them to him.

Shane opened the can and poured some into my hand. I stuffed them in my mouth and chewed while Shane watched my face.

"Well?" he asked.

"Definitely got an old taste to them," I said. "Kind of chewy, but not that bad."

We continued down the hall, stuffing our mouths with cashews until we'd eaten them all. I saw a faint line of light ahead of us. Shane must have seen it, too, because he quickened his pace and passed three more rooms without even looking into them. We came to a T in the passageway and looked right. Sunlight poured through a window not far from us. We approached the window and looked out over a network of pipes and steel making up the center of the rig. I looked for a way to open the window, but it was sealed shut. Shane tried the door to our left and it revealed another lounge area awash in sunlight.

I crossed the floor and slid the windows open with my elbows. I felt fresh Gulf air blow across my face and circulate through the stale room. The view looked out over the water.

"This works," Shane said.

I stood there for a moment, staring at the horizon and savoring the clean air.

"Look," Shane said. "A map."

I looked where he was pointing and saw a floor plan for the rig. A red dot marked our location as the THIRD FLOOR WEST LOUNGE. The diagram was complicated, with a confusing network of passageways and multiple levels encircling the drilling equipment in the center. Most of the first floor was utility space with supply rooms and engine housing. The second floor, where the galley was, appeared to be mostly living space. The third level was offices and meeting rooms. Shane came up behind me and peered over my shoulder. I put my finger on a small break room down the hall from us and another room past it marked COM-MUNICATIONS.

"Let's start with the break room," I said. "There may be more food."

The break room had a small refrigerator, a sink, and a few high-top tables and chairs. The refrigerator had a six-pack of bottled water. Shane grabbed them and put them under his arm. I searched the cabinets above the sink and found a case of granola bars. I tore one open and bit into it. It tasted like old cardboard and I spat it into the sink.

"Nope," I said.

"I guess we'll have to get that fishing equipment out of the lifeboats," Shane said.

"Or maybe there's an actual fishing rod in one of the bedrooms below," I said. "We can check later."

I looked in the last cabinet, found another first aid kit, and pulled it out. "I might need this," I said.

"Bring it," Shane said. "Let's go check the communications room and see what we find."

The communications room appeared to be the control center for the rig. There was a view over the derrick from behind a row of computers with large flat-screen monitors. On both sides of the room were racks of larger computers. I picked up a telephone handset next to one of the keyboards and heard nothing. I set it down, frustrated.

"All of this stuff is dead," I said. "Nothing's going to work without power."

"There's got to be something," he said.

"Well, there's nothing here."

We returned to the lounge and lay down on separate sofas. The soft cushions felt like the most comfortable bed I'd ever been on. Despite my frustration and the pain in my hands, it wasn't long before I crashed into sleep.

32

MY THROBBING HANDS EVENTUALLY WOKE ME AGAIN, AND I opened my eyes to stare at the water-stained ceiling tiles. Wind whistled across the rig and rain pattered the outside wall. I looked down at my watch. It read almost three o'clock. I'd been asleep for nearly five hours.

I looked over at Shane and saw him lying on his back with his eyes open.

"Did you even sleep?"

"Yeah," he said. "Like I was dead. The wind woke me."

The rain came harder and blew in through the windows and began to sprinkle us.

"Think we should close the windows?" Shane said.

I sat up. "No," I said. "It feels good. But let's scoot the sofas toward the middle of the room so they don't get wet."

I used my hips to help Shane push the sofas a few feet away from the windows. Then I sat down again, took off my gloves, and inspected my palms. The bandages were bloody and needed changing.

"That looks bad," Shane said.

I opened the first aid kit and took out what I needed. Then I removed the bandages and revealed my hands to him.

"Man," he winced. "You need stitches."

"Yeah," I said.

"So are you going to tell me what happened?"

I held my hands out in front of him. "Help me do this first before I lose my nerve. Grab that bottle of alcohol and pour it on."

"Are you serious?"

"Yeah, I'm serious. Barnacle cuts can get infected quick."

"You need something to bite on?"

I desperately wanted him to just stop talking and get it over with.

"No," I said. "Just pour it on my hands and get ready to hear me scream. It's gonna hurt bad."

Shane took off the top of the alcohol bottle and looked at me.

"Come on, will you?" I said. "And don't just trickle it out, pour it on good."

He shook his head, winced, and tilted the bottle. I screamed and lay back and writhed in pain.

"You okay?" Shane asked after a few minutes.

I stared at the ceiling and nodded. I could feel cold sweat sitting on my face.

"How many more times you going to do that?" he asked.

"I don't think I can do it again," I said. "Hopefully that's enough."

Shane helped me sit up and began redressing my hands. As he wrapped the gauze I told him how we'd floated against the mooring rope and how I'd climbed up the rig and lifted him with the winch.

He listened to it all without saying a word.

"I would have died for sure," he said after I was done.

I didn't answer him.

"You saved my life."

"Anybody else would have done the same thing," I said. "You can't leave people to die."

"I think Dad would have left me. If it came down to only one of us being able to live."

"No way."

"It's hard to believe, but that's really how he was."

"You don't know that."

Shane sighed. "Well, anyway, we're safe now."

"Just not exactly rescued," I said.

"What about the lifeboats?" Shane said. "You think we can float away in one?"

"Sure. But who knows how long we'd be drifting out there," I said. "We could die of thirst or starvation before anyone found us."

"Yeah," Shane said like he'd already thought the same thing. "We have to figure out how to call for help. From here."

I grabbed more bandages and stood.

"Where are you going?" Shane asked.

"I'm going into the hall to change the bandages on my legs."

"You got cut there, too?"

"Yeah," I said. "But not as bad."

After changing my bandages I came back inside and lay down. I didn't feel like talking about our problems anymore. I'd had enough for one day.

The rain moved on and the windows dripped and I heard the sound of waves against the understructure. I was so tired that I felt queasy, but my hands weren't letting me sleep. I rolled over and Shane looked at me. I stood and started toward the door.

"Where you going?" he asked.

"For a walk," I said. "Can't sleep."

I went down the hall to a door that led to a small lookout platform outside the control room. I sat against the railing, lowered my hands into my lap, and looked out over the steel confusion of the rig, dripping and dead. I felt like I'd been sent to an abandoned space station on another planet. And I couldn't help but think of my parents, hundreds of miles away.

33

ME AND MOM AND DAD WERE ALL PRETTY HAPPY ONCE. I THOUGHT of the times we were together doing simple things like walking on the beach or wheeling a grocery cart through the supermarket. Dad has a way of appearing awkward and out of place when he's not in a boat. He wears the same threadbare plaid shirts and khaki shorts and flip-flops no matter where we go. It takes him a while to get comfortable when you pull him away from the dive shop and the water. He's always making jokes as a way of covering it up. In the old days, Mom tried not to crack up at his comedy routine, but a slight smile at the edge of her mouth never failed to break into a laugh.

At the time it just seemed that was how it was supposed to be. Sometimes both of them could be so embarrassing and annoying, but nothing felt more right than when we were together.

For some reason I thought about a time we all visited Fort Morgan, a Civil War fort at the end of a peninsula not far from our home. Dad was driving his old pickup truck, Brownie. We had the windows down and I was sitting between Mom and Dad, feeling the breeze in my face. Mom always complained about Dad's truck because it smelled like a wet towel and the air conditioner didn't work. Dive equipment parts and pieces were scattered about the floor and stuffed behind the seats. But it was his smell and strong and healthy in its own way. And even though Mom sometimes complained, she did it with a smile, like there was something about it she secretly liked.

When we got to the fort Dad pulled a blanket out of the truck bed and told me to grab the cooler. He always carried a small Igloo cooler in the back along with jerricans of gasoline, fishing rods, propane tanks, and more dive equipment. The clutter drove me crazy and I was constantly trying to organize things, only to have him throw something else right into the middle of it. The Igloo was about the only thing that never slid around. I'd strapped it to the sidewall with a bungee cord so it wouldn't pour out. It was always full of something, like a portable refrigerator. The first thing Dad did each morning was stop at the convenience store and fill the cooler with soft drinks, bottled water, and ice. That day he'd picked up some sandwiches and a bag of potato chips, too.

"Grab your book and sun hat, doll," he said to Mom. "We got the rest handled."

I looked at Dad. "Fishing rods?" I whispered.

He glanced at Mom and back at me. "You can get one if you want, sweetheart. I think I'll enjoy your mother's company."

So I fished from the shore while they lay on the blanket under the shade of a weather-beaten live oak. I remembered glancing back at them from time to time. They were talking and laughing and it didn't seem like we needed anything else in the world. There was a magical pull between them that I felt but couldn't put into words. The pull seemed so strong that I couldn't imagine them ever being apart.

I returned to the lounge as the sun set outside the windows and darkness slipped over the room. I sat on the sofa, staring at my gloved hands. Shane lay on his back, looking up at the ceiling, magazines scattered on the floor beside him.

"It's getting dark in here," he said. "You want me to turn on the lantern?"

"No," I said. "Save the batteries."

"I've been thinking of what we can do," he said.

"I can't do much with these hands."

"They'll get better."

"I don't know," I said.

"As soon as we're rescued you can get stitches."

I nodded doubtfully and then both of us sat there without speaking as nightfall settled over us. Eventually all we had to see by was the glow of a starlit sky coming through the windows. The breeze remained steady out of the west and kept the room cool and comfortable.

"Maybe we'll find some decent food tomorrow," Shane eventually said.

"Yeah," I said.

"Maybe some survival rations off the lifeboats."

"Sure," I said. I didn't want to tell Shane my concerns. I wanted to stay positive. But I already had a bad feeling that we'd just escaped one survival situation only to find ourselves in another, entirely different one.

34

I WAS ABLE TO SLEEP UNTIL THE EARLY MORNING HOURS, WHEN
my hands woke me. The breeze had died, and the air was
hot and still. My face was sticky with sweat and my mouth
was dry. I stared across the dark room, listening to the
steady breathing of Shane and the dead silence of the rig
with the water pounding it far below. It was strange to be
near an open window and not hear the whine of mosquitoes. Above the water, there was nothing alive for a
hundred miles. Not even a fly.

I got some ibuprofen and took it with a few swigs of
water. Then I was able to fall asleep again. When I opened

my eyes the room was lighter and Shane was standing over me.

"I'm going to get some of those survival rations out of the lifeboat. You wanna come?"

I sat up and brushed my hair behind my ears. "Yeah," I said.

I grabbed my booties and tried to pull them on, but the pain in my hands made me clench my jaw.

"Here," Shane said.

He knelt in front of me and tugged the booties on and zipped them. It was a relief to finally have Shane be helpful.

"Thanks," I said. "I won't be able to carry much, but I can put a few things under my arms."

It wasn't long before we were standing before the lifeboats again. Shane climbed inside the closest one and returned with a bag of chocolate and energy bars. We sat on the deck and ate small portions of each. The chocolate tasted fine, but the energy bars tasted like bland oatmeal.

"Hopefully there's something else in the galley that we can eat," I said. "That's not spoiled."

"Got to be," Shane said, chewing slowly.

"It's going to be tough eating this stuff every day."

"Yeah," he agreed. "It's pretty bad."

After our small meal we decided to explore more of the rig. We continued past the stairwell to a solid steel door. Shane pulled on the handle, but it didn't give.

He passed the lantern to me, gripped the handle with both hands, and jerked. The door popped loose and creaked open. The smell of oil and rust and wetness floated over us. He reached back for the light and I pressed it into his hand. Then he shone it over the room and revealed a massive network of pipes and control panels and gauges. Much of it was rusty and glistening with oil and condensation.

"You first," he whispered over his shoulder.

I elbowed him in the back. "Shut up," I hissed. "You've got the light."

"I'm glad your fists don't work," he said.

"You're never going to stop talking about that, are you?"

"Well, you did punch me in the face. Hard."

I shoved him again. "Go. I can still save up until my fists feel better again."

He started forward and I lightly pinched the back of his shirt and held on to him. We made our way across the slippery floor. Shane passed the light over pipes and computer screens and discarded tools and workbenches with open notebooks on them. The room seemed to go on in all directions with no clear exit.

"You going to remember how to get out of here?" I whispered.

"Yeah. I think so."

"There's got to be a working flashlight somewhere."

"Maybe, but I doubt it. This lantern had a tab I had to pull to activate the batteries. It probably kept them fresh."

Rising out of the darkness was an enormous piece of machinery.

"There's the generator," I said. "Probably powers this whole rig."

We walked close and stopped and studied it.

"Think we can start it?" Shane asked.

"I wouldn't even know where to begin," I said. "Something this big. And I'm sure it needs some oil or something after five years."

"I was just kidding," Shane said.

"Let's go back to the second floor," I said. "It seems like that's where most of the people lived. This is just a lot of tools and machinery down here."

everything behind, but more like they'd packed just what they needed and didn't return.

We chose a bunk room to move into and opened the windows to let it air out. The top bunk had a ladder that was easy to step up and I requested to sleep there. Shane said he was fine with the bottom. Then we walked down the hall, opening all the bedroom doors and windows to get as much fresh air and light as we could.

"Hey," Shane called to me.

I found him looking into a door we hadn't explored. There was a Ping-Pong table and a pool table and a soda machine. I crossed the floor and opened the windows while Shane tried to stick his hand up inside the drink machine.

"No way," I said.

He gave up and kicked it. "Even a *hot* Coke would be good," he said.

We couldn't get our hands on any soft drinks, but we found some Gatorade powder in the galley and combined it in a jug with bottled water. We sat on the floor and passed it back and forth, spilling it over our mouths and savoring the sugary sweetness. We drank the entire jug, mixed more, and took it back to the makeshift pantry in our bedroom.

That evening we watched the sun set from the helicopter pad while eating chocolate bars and drinking

35

WE INVESTIGATED MORE OF THE SECOND DECK AND FOUND AN entire hallway of bedrooms along the west side that had windows overlooking the water. Some of the mattresses had sheets and pillows. A few of the bedside tables had family pictures still on them, and closets had clothes on hangers. We found books and stationery and medicine cabinets full of things like half-empty toothpaste tubes and razors.

"This is so weird," Shane said.

It was weird. And spooky. It felt like we were the last survivors on earth, picking through people's lost personal effects. It didn't appear they'd hurried out and left

Gatorade. A cool, salty breeze swept across our faces and played with our hair. Miles away, a dark cloud prowled over the gulf, dragging its veil of rain.

"It just doesn't make sense to go through what we did only to get stuck here like this," Shane said.

"How long do you think the lifeboat rations will last?" I asked.

"A couple of weeks, maybe."

"We'll need to make an SOS signal," I said. "Up on the helipad."

"You think anybody ever flies this way?"

"We've got to do *something*," I said.

Shane nodded.

"We'll find some paint down below and make the sign tomorrow," I said.

Thunder rumbled again.

"You think there's more storms out here than on the shore?" Shane asked.

"No," I said. "But it seems like it. It's just easier to see and hear them."

Shane looked at me. "I'm sorry I was such a wimp."

"What are you talking about?" I said.

"You know, in the water. After the anchor pulled."

"You weren't a wimp. You were scared. You didn't know anything about it."

"I saw the anchor," he said. "I knew something wasn't right."

"We both did, but who would imagine it would turn into this?"

"We should have waited on you."

"We all made mistakes," I said.

Shane didn't answer me.

"I've been in that water more times than I can count," I continued. "And the more you do it, the more you realize that you're just a guest. You can't really control any of it. You have to get in there quietly and get out and hope you don't make her mad."

"Who?"

"Mother Nature."

Something splashed in the water far below us. We crawled to the edge of the platform and peered down. The surface crackled and popped with bait fish and the dark shapes of larger fish moving in and out of the rig structure.

"You think we could eat them raw?" he said.

"The tuna for sure," I said.

"You think there's tuna down there?"

"Yeah," I said. "And you can probably eat lots of other fish raw. This water's so clean I don't think it would hurt you."

"But we still have more of the rig to explore. Maybe

we'll find some way to signal for help before it comes to that."

"Yeah," I said. "Maybe so."

That night was hard. In addition to my hands hurting, nightmares played in my head like little horror movies. All the visions had to do with my parents finding me on the rig but not recognizing me or a search party arriving but not being able to locate us. I tossed and turned, trying to sleep, but I couldn't get out from under the bad dreams like they hung in the air itself, as though the rig was full of them. The worst part of it all was waking and thinkings that these nightmares, unlike any I'd had before, had actually happened.

36

AS SUNLIGHT CREPT OVER THE ROOM, I HUNG MY HEAD OVER THE edge of the top bunk and watched Shane's face, waiting for him to wake. After my night of terrible visions I desperately wanted to hear his voice.

"Shane," I finally said.

He opened his eyes.

"Let's go make the SOS sign," I said.

"Okay," he said.

We went downstairs to locate some paint. We found three spray cans of orange Rust-Oleum in the storage room and took them back up to the helipad. We started at opposite ends of the pad and made our SOS signal.

Each letter was nearly fifteen feet tall and we figured a plane or helicopter could see it from miles away.

I felt better once we had the SOS sign working for us. For added measure we also got the flares from the lifeboats and brought them up to our bedroom. If by chance we happened to see a passing plane or ship, it would be good to have them centrally located.

So far, all of our exploration had been focused on the rooms on the outside edges of the rig. Shane wanted to see the derrick up close, so we went downstairs again to find our way to the center. We exited a rear door of the generator room and emerged with the derrick looming a hundred feet overhead. We approached it and wandered about its base, inspecting the giant cables and hardware used to handle the drilling pipe. After a moment we got up the nerve to step beneath it and peer down through the drilling hole at the waves below. Wind came from under the platform and up through the opening to blow across our faces.

"I wonder if there's still a hole down there," Shane said.

I backed away. "Come on," I said. "I'm done hauling you out of the water."

Shane followed me and looked up at the derrick. A steel ladder was welded to the support beams in staggered twenty-foot sections. Each section was connected with a narrow platform that seemed designed for a climber to stop and rest.

"How'd you like to have to climb that thing?" I said.

The backdrop of passing clouds against the tower made it appear to sway in a way that made me dizzy.

"I wouldn't," he said.

We wandered about the drilling area, picking up old tools and kicking at bits of trash left behind years ago. We didn't find anything we thought was helpful, so we eventually returned to our room upstairs. We ate a quick snack before Shane went to look for fishing equipment and I set about cleaning up, determined to rid our space of five years of dust and grime.

I put on some rubber gloves I'd found in the kitchen, got an old towel, and attempted to wipe some of the mildew off the furniture and the walls with Clorox and water. I was able to remove some of it, but most, especially around the ceiling and the floor, was too thick and it hurt my hands to apply much pressure. But just the little bit I was able to do made the place feel cleaner.

An hour later Shane returned with a fishing rod and tackle box that he'd found in a utility closet on the other side of the rig. We took the equipment to the mooring platform and cast a spinner bait. A large fish flashed through the water and attacked it immediately. Shane tried to reel it up but the weight broke it off.

"This fishing line's too old and brittle," he said.

I recalled watching shark fishermen on the public pier in Gulf Shores and how they hoisted their catch.

"Got an idea," I said.

I found a laundry basket and had Shane tie the winch rope to it in a way that we could drop it to the water. The next fish we caught he pulled into the basket and I winched it up from above. In a moment we had a thirty-pound jack crevalle flipping about on the platform. Shane and I gave each other a high five to celebrate the team-work.

Jacks are especially bloody fish, and I didn't want to eat it raw. I sent Shane to get matches from one of the life-boats, a large pot and a grill from the galley, and some paper to burn. Meanwhile I used my dive knife to clean the fish.

When Shane returned I had several filets on a plastic tarp before me and my cloth gloves were ruined with blood. We made a fire in the pot and lay the strips on the grill. As the paper burned it floated up and stuck to the fish, and soon the meat was covered in black ash. It was clear that our grill wasn't going to work without wood or charcoal.

"We can break up some furniture and burn it," Shane said.

"How many matches do we have?" I asked.

"I found about twenty in one of the boats. There's probably that many in the other one."

I cut away a sliver of meat and brushed the ash off with my glove.

"Forty matches won't last us long anyway," I said.

"I'm sure there's a cigarette lighter or something around here."

"Maybe," I said. "Maybe not. Then we need lighter fluid. "

I held the glistening bloody sliver up before my face.

"That's nasty," Shane said.

"Here goes," I said.

He watched with a disgusted look on his face as I lowered the meat onto my tongue. I chewed slowly and let the strong coppery taste of fish blood fill my mouth. Then I closed my eyes and swallowed quickly.

"How is it?" Shane asked.

I opened my eyes. "Not great," I said. "But not too bad."

Shane ate a sliver and agreed that it wasn't good, but it wasn't the worst thing he'd ever eaten. And it seemed more practical than trying to build a fire every time we wanted to have meat.

I grabbed some shop towels from the storage room and we both ate more of the raw jack crevalle, wiping the blood from the edges of our mouths. When we'd had our fill we tossed the rest of the fish overboard, since there was no way to keep it from spoiling. Then I threw my gloves over the railing after them. I'd get more from the storage room on the way back upstairs.

37

OVER THE NEXT FEW DAYS WE CONTINUED TO EXPLORE THE RIG, hoping to find more water, better food, and some means of communication with the outside world.

Shane eventually found the tank for the rig's supply of fresh water. It was drained and empty. That got us thinking about having something to drink once the bottled water was gone. We gathered all the pots and pans we could out of the galley and placed them outside to collect rainwater. Then we got all the bottled waters we could find from the lifeboats and scattered throughout the rig and carried them to our room and inventoried them. We counted a hundred and eighty twenty-ounce bottles. It sounded like a lot, but if we limited ourselves to just three bottles each per day, that was only about a month's worth. And the way things were looking, it was likely we'd be on the rig at least that long.

Water didn't worry me. It was lack of food and no hope of rescue that fueled my nightmares and kept me up at night. Most of the food we found was spoiled, and without power we couldn't get any of the electronics working. We identified several generators throughout the rig, but even if the engines had remnants of fuel in them, they were giant and complicated and intimidating. We thought about the *Deepwater Horizon* disaster and feared that we'd start a fire if we tampered with any of it.

After a week it seemed we'd been through every part of the rig and we were no closer to finding a way off. I found a calendar in one of the offices and brought it back to our bedroom. I hung it on the wall and marked off the days we'd been gone. Since the calendar was five years old, the exact days didn't match, but it gave me some sense of passing time.

We used the restroom outside and over the edge of the walkways. There wasn't enough water to waste on showers so I had to get used to the parched feel and sour smell of dried sweat on my skin. My hair was stiff and salty and felt like a dirty mop on my head. I could get past the thought of using someone else's old toothbrush, but I felt foolish wasting water on my teeth too. I got an old stick of Axe deodorant from one of the medicine cabinets and occasionally wiped my underarms with it just to feel a little clean.

In addition to nightmares and bouts of depression, we fought boredom. In the recreation room we found a cabinet with DVDs, decks of cards, and checkers. It was hard for me to handle cards, so Shane and I spent a lot of time playing checkers and talking.

We had nothing better to do, and after all we'd been through, sharing personal things wasn't a big deal.

"I'm not going to worry about my parents anymore," I said to him one day.

"What's wrong with them?"

"I don't know. I don't think even *they* know. They're just not happy."

"Were they happy before the divorce?"

"I thought so. It all happened so fast. I always thought it was because of Dad and the stupid Malzon tanks. Now I think it had to have been a lot more than that. There must be stuff I don't know about."

"Sometimes people just end up not liking each other. Like my parents."

"Dad's frustrating, but there's no way not to like him. And I know he still loves Mom."

"Maybe she doesn't love him."

"She does. But she can't admit it. She's stubborn like that."

Shane watched me and didn't answer.

"But I know now that I can't make them happy. They're going to have to figure it out."

Shane continued to study me. "You think I'm selfish for not missing my dad?"

"No," I said. "But that's different. It sounds like he wasn't nice to you or your mom."

"It's like he had me in this hole I couldn't climb out of, and every time I tried he kept shoveling dirt on me. Why would anybody be like that? He was supposed to help me and give me good advice. You know, stuff like that."

I shook my head to indicate that I didn't have an answer.

"I used to be really mad about going to boarding school," he said. "Like my parents were just throwing me away."

"But you're not now?"

He shook his head. "No," he said. "I can start over with people I don't know."

"You've already got a lot going for you."

"I'm pretty good at sports."

"You're good at a lot of things."

Shane smiled to himself and moved a game piece.

"Don't let it go to your head," I said. "You need a haircut."

He looked at me. "Why don't you cut it for me?"

I held up my hands.

"Oh, yeah," he said.

"But when they're better," I continued, "that'll be the first thing I do."

I didn't really want to cut his hair. His long hair was part of the Shane I'd come to know.

"I'll write you," I said. "At your new school."

"It's not like I won't come home."

"Then I'll write you and visit when you come home," I said. "Make sure you're still being nice."

Shane looked down at the board and frowned. "Will you stop with that?" he said.

"Yeah," I said. "I was just kidding."

He looked up at me again and smiled weakly. I was sorry for what I'd said.

"Hopefully we'll get back before school starts," I said.

"But what if we don't?"

I shook my head. "I don't know."

"What if we have to spend the winter here?"

I didn't answer. I'd thought about it, but it depressed me too much to discuss.

"Think how cold it's going to get," Shane said.

"Let's don't talk about it," I answered.

38

WE CONTINUED TO EAT THE SURVIVAL RATIONS FROM THE lifeboats and watch our supply of food slowly dwindle. I knew we could catch fish again when we needed to, but I was putting it off as long as possible. It was a lot of work, and the thought of eating more bloody jack crevalle made me queasy.

Getting water didn't seem to be a problem. Shane located an empty barrel that looked like it once held potable water. He rolled it outside onto the deck and we emptied our pots of rainwater into it.

As the days passed, though, I found it harder and harder

to motivate myself to do anything. Sometimes it was all I could do just to make myself get up and eat and drink. And when I did, it only reminded me of our rations getting slowly depleted. We didn't talk about it much, but both of us had all but given up on finding anything else of value on the rig. Now we were simply planning to live a life of survival hibernation.

One evening Shane suggested we go up to the helipad and shoot flares.

"Why?" I said.

"I've just been wanting to do it. I've always wanted to shoot one. And who knows, maybe somebody will see it. At least it's something."

"Sure," I said. "I've always wanted to shoot one, too."

We took two hand flares up to the helipad. Shane took one of them and approached the edge of the platform. He pulled the cap and pointed it overhead. The flare sparked at the end before shooting an orange fireball into the sky. The ball traveled high and hung there for a moment before starting a slow fall toward the water. It was so big and bright that it seemed impossible no one else could see it. But I knew we were alone. And the fireball eventually drifted down into the waves and disappeared. Then I shot mine and watched it do the same.

We ate the last of the chocolate and energy bars on the thirteenth day. From that point forward our only possible food was going to be raw fish and spoiled canned goods.

"We have to figure out how to dry the fish meat," I said. "Like pioneers. We've got to figure out some way to build up a supply so we don't have to fish every day."

"I guess we just leave it in the sun," Shane said.

"Seems like it would spoil," I said. "Don't you smoke it first?"

"Do I look like Daniel Boone to you?"

I wasn't in the mood for sarcasm. "Don't be a smart-ass," I said.

"I don't know," Shane said. "I guess we'll just have to try."

That afternoon we caught a ten-pound amberjack and hoisted it up in the basket. Once I cut into the fish I saw the meat squirming with tapeworms.

"Can we eat it?" Shane asked.

"I think so," I said. "If we get the worms out."

"I can't believe something can live with that many parasites," Shane said.

"I know," I said. "But lots of fish have them."

I spent nearly an hour pulling and cutting the worms

out and flicking them over the side. Finally I sliced the filets into thin, almost translucent strips and hung them over the railing to dry in the sun. It was hard to imagine they'd turn into anything more than rancid fish meat.

As if depleting our food supply wasn't bad enough, that evening we faced another problem that was just as serious. As we got ready to play our nightly game of checkers the lantern began to flicker. Shane had the one from the other lifeboat ready to use, but when he pulled the activation tab and flipped the switch nothing happened.

Shane shook the lantern. "How can it not work?" he said.

I got a sick feeling just thinking about not having light.

Shane unscrewed the bottom of the lantern and peered inside it. "Crap," he said. "It's corroded."

There was nothing to do but go to bed early.

Our first night without any light was the longest we'd faced. Between bad dreams I lay on my back staring into the grainy darkness and checking my watch. I thought it would never end.

When daylight finally crept across the bedroom floor Shane and I got up and used the last bit of lantern power to prepare for the dark nights ahead. We tied ropes together and strung them from the top of the stairwell down to the outside of the storage room so that we could find our way downstairs. Then we did the same up to the third level and out to the helipad. We got the remaining matches from the lifeboats and placed a few in the bedroom and the rest in the storage room for emergency purposes. By the time we were done the lantern gave off nothing more than a faint orange glow. We shut it off to be used in an emergency only.

That afternoon we checked on the fish meat. It was stiffening up like cardboard. I bent close and smelled it.

"Not bad," I said. "Actually smells better than when it was raw."

"Well, there's no flies to get on it," he said. "And no birds to steal it."

Shane lifted a piece off the railing and bit into it. He looked at me while he chewed. "It's better," he said. "I think this is going to work."

I took the meat from him and tasted it. It was definitely less fishy tasting, but it was still a little slimy and bloody.

"Needs to dry more," I said, "but, yeah, it's better."

It seemed we had the worst of our problems figured out. We had a way to gather water, a plan to stockpile food, and a system to overcome navigating the rig in darkness. Now all we had to do was wait for someone to find us.

But there was an even bigger problem we'd never considered. A problem that had been haunting us all along.

39

WE'D BEEN ON THE RIG THREE WEEKS WHEN SHANE BEGAN TO cough. At first we didn't take it seriously. But after two more days the cough grew deep and raspy and he became weak and pale. He didn't feel like getting out of bed or eating.

"It's probably just a cold," I told him.

Shane agreed, but even then I don't think either of us really believed it. It didn't make sense catching a cold when there was no one to catch it from.

I gave him ibuprofen and some cough syrup I found in a medicine cabinet, but it didn't seem to help.

"Do you think I've got the flu or something?" he asked.

"I don't know," I said.

"I think the flu comes from animals. Like birds and pigs. There's nothing out here. Not even seagulls."

"We don't know it's the flu. It could be something else. Maybe a virus that's been living here for five years."

"I'll bet it got bored," Shane said, smiling at his joke.

"And tired of the food," I said, laughing.

Shane chuckled and sighed. Neither of us spoke for a moment.

"You think we could make it a year or two?" he finally said.

I thought about it and nodded. "We could, but I think I might go crazy."

"It would be like our lives just stopped. All the school we'd miss. Everybody getting older and forgetting about us."

"Somebody has to come," I said.

Shane nodded, but I sensed he didn't believe my words any more than I did.

Over the next week Shane's condition didn't improve. The only thing that made him feel better was sitting outside, breathing the fresh air, and feeling the breezes on his face. Each day I helped him take a blanket, a pillow, and water upstairs and onto the lookout where part of the rig extended about ten feet overhead. This small roof created shelter from the sun, but it wasn't enough to keep rain from blowing in. I tied one of the emergency blankets to the railing to help keep him dry during afternoon squalls.

I kept the water pots emptied into the barrel and tried to fish some. Without Shane to help me, I couldn't use the basket and most of what I caught broke the line. Sometimes I managed to reel up a small bluefish or a lane snapper, and these were more than enough for what we needed, especially with Shane's loss of appetite.

When I sat there next to him it felt like there was nothing left to say, but occasionally we still found small thoughts and pieces of our lives that we shared.

"I've been thinking about Mom," he said to me one day.

"What about her?"

"About what a pain my dad and I both were."

I didn't respond.

"I wonder if she still loves me."

"Of course she does."

"I think she's got a boyfriend," he said.

"What?"

"I caught her talking on her phone once outside the back door. She was whispering, and she acted really weird when she saw me."

"What was she saying?"

"I couldn't really tell."

"Is she gone a lot?" I asked.

"Yeah, all the time."

"Do you think your dad knew?"

"Maybe. He didn't act like it. But he never seemed to care what she did."

I didn't respond.

"I wonder if she's with her boyfriend," Shane continued. "I hope she is. I mean, especially now."

"Maybe you'll meet him when we get home."

"Yeah," Shane said. "When I get home."

Each morning I marked off another date on the calendar and helped Shane carry his things upstairs to the lookout. I checked on him throughout the day, bringing him new magazines, water, and fish. Sometimes I was able to convince him to eat something, but mostly he just wanted to sit there and stare over the rig. This left me alone for hours at a time, lying in our bedroom, mostly sleeping. Sleep during the day was the only thing that really brought me any peace. I didn't have so many nightmares, and it seemed to be the only time that I could close my eyes and dream my way off our island prison.

40

DAY THIRTY-ONE. I WAS ALONE, READING IN MY BED, WHEN I
coughed. The sudden impulse and sound of it froze me.
After a moment I made myself cough again and felt a
scratchy feeling in my throat.

I put my book down and sat up and let the dead silence of the rig press in on me.

I've got it.

And it wasn't until then that I knew what we were up
against. It had been living on the rig all along.

I looked up at the sagging, stained ceiling tiles of our
bedroom and studied the black splotches creeping around
the edges. I looked at the baseboards and the doorjambs.

The black stains seemed to appear everywhere, like more had seeped in and spread during the night. I thought about the rig, closed up and warm and damp for so many years.

I made my way upstairs and onto the lookout and sat down next to Shane. He smiled at me through his woozy fog of boredom. I stared over the rusty steel and peeling paint of the rig. Suddenly it all looked diseased.

"It's the air in there," I said. "It's mold making us sick."

"What do you mean?"

"I've got it, too."

"Mold?"

I looked at him and nodded. "I coughed. I felt it."

"But we opened the windows," he said. "We let the fresh air in. You cleaned."

"It's not enough. We had it in the dive shop after Hurricane Katrina flooded the building. I remember a scratchy feeling in my throat and my eyes watering. We had to take out the walls and remove all the insulation to get rid of it."

Shane looked away. It seemed like he was trying to think of something to say, some way to argue with me. But there was no argument.

"Stay out here with me," he said. "It helps."

"We can't live out here."

"Just until we feel better," he finally said.

"I don't think we're going to get better," I said. "The stuff's alive inside us," I said. "All in our throats and chest. We've been breathing it for weeks."

"What do you think it does?"

"I don't know. And I don't know how to get rid of it. But we can't sleep inside there anymore."

"We can make a tent outside the storage room," Shane continued. "There's a big area of covered space down there."

"At least with the bedroom I sort of remembered what it was like to live in a real house. Now we have to make a tent on a hard steel floor. What about when winter comes? What about the storms?"

"Maybe mold's not down in the storage room."

I sighed. "Maybe not."

We sat there without speaking for a while, watching the giant cloud shadows move across the sky. I remembered my nightmarish thoughts of being starved, then dead and picked at by seagulls.

"When do we give up, Julie?" he said.

"I don't know," I said. "Maybe you can't even if you want to."

We moved two mattresses down to a small alcove outside the storage room. Shane barely had the energy to help, but there was no way I could have done it without him. It was on that same day that I stopped marking the calendar.

The days continued to pass. Occasionally I got up and fished and put more meat out to dry on the railing. But most of the time we spent simply lying on the mattresses, doing nothing, saying nothing. Now not only were the nights long, but the days were, too, as we watched the squalls prowl over the Gulf and the cloud shadow and the schools of feeding fish. The rest of the world was going on a hundred miles away like it had given us up for dead and forgotten us.

Sometimes the rain swept over us. Our new bedroom offered enough cover overhead to keep it from blowing in, but water still ran across the steel floor and wicked up into our mattresses. I eventually wrapped them in plastic tarps, which kept them dry but also made them hot and uncomfortable. The thought of lying on an exposed steel deck eating dried fish and drinking rainwater indefinitely was almost impossible to bear.

41

AT FIRST IT LOOKED LIKE NOTHING MORE THAN ANOTHER afternoon squall, grumbling and flickering far away to the west. But after a while the bruised line of clouds began to consume the entire horizon, and soon it was obvious that we were watching the approach of a storm that was bigger than any we'd seen. And it appeared we were directly in its path.

I emptied all the pots into the water barrel and repositioned them near the edge of the railing. Not a moment later, the rig fell into shadow and we felt cool gusts of wind blow over us. Soon the Gulf water began to whitecap and spot with rain. From our small alcove we watched lightning strobe against the swells and heard thunder slamming after it like a steel gate. Rain began to pelt the side of the rig in windblown sheets, and I felt the mist of it on my face.

"We may get wet this time," I said.

Shane didn't answer me. I looked over and saw him staring intently out into the weather. I searched for what he was looking at and it only took me a moment to see it. Through the haze of gray was a giant wavering cone of darkness dropping out of the clouds and drilling the surface of the water into a white froth. Then I heard it, rumbling like a train, vibrating the steel beneath me.

"Holy crap," Shane muttered.

"Waterspout!" I yelled.

Shane was already starting to stand. "Get inside!" he said.

I stood and grabbed his arm and shoved him into the storage room. I slammed the door behind us and locked it. Then I held on to him in the inky darkness as he felt his way along the guide rope. In a moment we came to the stairs. Shane sat down, and I sat beside him and grabbed and squeezed his hand. We felt the rig shaking and creaking and groaning, and we heard the howl and shriek of the waterspout as it tried to twist and tear the structure to pieces.

"Holy crap," Shane said again.

Something loud crashed outside like a part of the structure had toppled over. There was clattering and banging all around us. I was too terrified to move or speak. We stayed there, squeezed together in the stairwell for what seemed like ten minutes but what was probably only thirty seconds. Then, suddenly, there was no more howling and shrieking. We listened to the waterspout as it rumbled off to the east. And the only sound was that of the wind and rain pelting the outside walls again.

"I think it's gone," I said.

"You think it hit the rig?" Shane asked.

"If it didn't, then it had to have brushed it," I said. "You could feel this whole thing shaking."

"Come on," Shane said. "Let's go look outside."

We made our way back to the door, unlocked it, and stepped into the alcove. It was almost night, and I could barely see. The first thing I noticed was that the mattresses were gone. Then I realized the deck was completely clean, like we'd never been there.

"No!" I cried.

I rushed out into the rain and looked down to where

our water pots had been. They were gone. The water barrel was gone. All the dried fish were gone. Even our fishing equipment had been blown away.

Shane came up behind me. "That was everything," he said blankly. "That was everything we had."

I couldn't answer him. I was in shock.

"Now we're really going to die," he said.

42

THE ALCOVE WAS SO WET AFTER THE WATERSPOUT THAT WE moved into the storage room for the rest of the night. I left the steel door open and the small amount of light coming from outside was all we had to orient ourselves. Otherwise it was so dark that I couldn't see my hands before my face.

I felt my way over to the shelves and pulled down the box of uniforms. I changed into one and took Shane another one.

"I don't know what size it is," I said. "But it's dry."

"Thanks," he said.

Shane took the uniform and moved away to change.

I poured the rest of the box onto the floor for something soft to sleep on.

In spite of our makeshift nest of uniforms, for the first time since we'd been on the rig I slept through the entire night. I didn't have any nightmares and I didn't lie awake worried about anything. I was resigned to the fact that Shane and I were going to die soon and now no amount of worrying and effort was going to save us.

The next day I woke to the rain still pattering the outside of the rig. Shane was already awake, lying on his back, staring at nothing.

"How do you feel?" I asked him.

"Not good," he said.

"Can you help me get new mattresses?"

"Yeah," he said. "I think so."

We dragged two more mattresses down to the storage room. Then Shane rested while I found a couple of flower vases and wastebaskets and set them out on the deck to catch rainwater. An hour later the wastebaskets had blown overboard. Then I found a steel bucket of bolts, dumped it out, and set it under the eaves.

In addition to the real sickness I had in my lungs, a mental sickness had taken over and it was hard to motivate myself to do anything. For a while I stood in the rain, watching the containers catching drips of rainwater, still in disbelief that our luck could be so bad. Finally I went and lay down next to Shane.

That afternoon I began to feel pangs of hunger and I knew I couldn't just lie there and starve.

"Where'd you find the fishing equipment?" I asked Shane. "Maybe there's more."

He sat up slowly. "That was it," he said. "But there's some fishing stuff in the lifeboats. It's not much, but it's something."

The lifeboats were tricky to get in and out of. Because of my injured hands, Shane had always considered it his job to get anything out of them.

"You think you can do it?" I asked him.

Shane sighed. "Yeah," he said. "I think so."

Shane climbed into both lifeboats and brought out the fishing kits. They were nothing more than two packages of monofilament line, a couple of hooks, four lures, two weights, and a plastic winder. It was the bare basics needed to catch a fish. I stared at the packages doubtfully.

"This might work for a couple of days," I said. "Maybe."

"It says there's only twelve feet of line in each kit," Shane said. "We'll have to tie the line to the end of a rope or something."

I closed my eyes and rubbed them. I said, "If we had a decent light I'd go back into the galley and search through everything. There's got to be some food that's not expired. Surely we missed something."

"Well, we don't have a light," he said. "We can't see a thing back there."

"I have a feeling spoiled food is all we'll have in a few days. I guess I'll have to make a torch or something to get to it. We've still got a few matches, don't we?"

"Yeah," Shane said. "But what if the canned food makes us sicker?"

I shrugged. "At this point, what would it matter?"

Shane didn't answer me. I desperately wanted him to encourage me to keep trying, but he wasn't going to. I lay down next to him again and listened to the endless rain drumming on the rig like it had moved over us to stay. My stomach groaned and knotted with hunger. And one more day slowly slipped into darkness.

43

WHEN I WAS IN SIXTH GRADE OUR TEACHER HAD US WATCH A video of six kids playing basketball. Three of the kids were wearing black and three were wearing white. The teacher told us to pay close attention and count how many times the kids in white passed the ball to each other. I counted sixteen times and that was the correct answer. However, what none of us noticed was that during the video a person in a gorilla suit walks onto the court, stands in the middle of the basketball players, and waves his hands around. It's strange how sometimes you can be so focused on the details around you that you miss what's right in front of you.

Shane mentioned starting a fire that night, and we came to realize something we'd both missed.

"Start a fire where?" I asked him. "It's been raining out there for almost two days."

"We could do it in here. In a bucket or something. I'd just feel better if we had some light."

"Do what you want," I said.

"It's just so dark. I think I'm going crazy."

"The light on the derrick is probably still going," I said. "It must have a battery and a solar charger. I wish there was some way to get it and bring it down."

Shane didn't speak right away.

Then, in a strange, contemplative way, he said, "The derrick."

"Yeah," I said. "Even that red light would be better than nothing."

"That's it," he said with rising excitement. "It's the derrick."

I tried to look at him through the darkness, but there was only black nothing before me. "What are you talking about?"

"It was right there all along, Julie. The light at the top of the derrick is our way out."

"How?"

"It's got to stay on. If we took out that light they'd have to come replace it. It's the law. Dad had a plane, and he talked about hazard beacons. They're all monitored."

"You mean we have to get up there and break it?"

"Right."

After all we'd been through, it was hard for me to believe anything was so simple. And it only took me a moment of consideration before I saw how impossible it was.

"But you're sick and my hands are worthless."

"I have to," he said. "It's my turn to do something."

"You can barely stand."

"We're dead if I don't."

"I might be able to," I said.

"No way," he said. "You have trouble just climbing into the lifeboats."

I knew he was right. "Even if you can get up there, it just can't be that simple."

"It is," Shane said. I had never heard him sound so confident.

"Okay," I said. "Tomorrow after it stops raining. You can try."

"No," he said. "Now. Who knows how I'll feel tomorrow?"

"We can't see to get through the generator room," I said.

"Go get the lantern," he said. "We'll use what's left of it."

Shane was so determined to climb the derrick that I didn't see any way to talk him out of it. And even if I had seen a way, I didn't want to. While I was still doubtful that his plan would work, I needed hope. And his idea, no matter how unlikely, was something to give us hope again and keep us moving.

I went up the guide ropes and got the lantern out of the bedroom. To save what little was left of the batteries, I didn't click it on until I was standing in the storage room again. Then I saw Shane already up and leaning against the shelving.

"You ready?" I said.

"Yeah," he said. "Let's do it."

44

I GATHERED THE LAST OF OUR MATCHES THAT WE'D STASHED ON one of the shelves for emergencies. I put them in my pocket so that we could use them to get back once the lantern failed. Then we set out down the hall.

The lantern was almost completely out by the time we reached the back of the generator room. I stopped, got the matches out of my pocket, and placed them on a small table. Then Shane pushed open the steel door and we faced the drizzling night. We heard the breeze whistling through the derrick structure and looked up to see the red light glowing almost a hundred feet overhead. He bent down and grabbed a crescent wrench with a rubber grip that was leaning against the wall.

"Something to break the light with," he said.

Part of me didn't even want to try. If it wasn't going to work, I didn't want to know. Not yet. I wanted to hold on to the hope just a little longer.

"We don't have to do this now," I said.

Shane slid the wrench into his pocket and coughed. "Yeah," he said. "We do."

And in that moment the lantern went out and left us standing there in the dark. But it wasn't as dark here as inside the rig. I could see Shane's silhouette, and there was something comforting about the red light blinking above.

I followed Shane to the edge of the derrick, where he grabbed hold of the ladder and started up, his feet falling heavily on the iron steps. And it was only a moment later that I felt like there should have been more to say. That I should have told him to be careful or something like that.

"Shane," I called after him.

The footfalls stopped. "What?" he said.

"Be careful," I said. "It's going to be slippery."

"Okay," he said.

"Go slow. Rest if you need to."

Shane continued climbing and I felt right again. I backed

away and stared up after him until he disappeared into the grainy darkness. The whistling breeze soon covered the sound of his footfalls.

I stared at the light blinking on and off and on and off. For what seemed like a half hour I stood there wiping the water from my face and looking for some sign of Shane. I finally saw a blurred outline of him blocking out the red glow. It seemed impossible that he was so high, and it made me nervous just thinking about it. He seemed to hesitate there for several minutes like he was resting. Then I noticed him shift, and a second later I heard a dull banging sound. I assumed he was hitting the light with the wrench. Several times the sound came to me, but the light kept glowing. And then he appeared to rest again.

"Forget it, Shane," I said to myself. "Come down."

The light glowed again and I saw that Shane had repositioned himself. The next bang I heard was louder, and orange and white sparks flew into the air around Shane's head. The beacon didn't glow again, and I heard the tinkle of glass shower the deck in front of me.

"Wahoo!" I yelled up at him.

I wasn't convinced the plan would work. Still, I couldn't help but feel a surge of excitement.

The only reply I got was the sound of the wind. Now, with the beacon gone, the rig had never looked and felt so dark.

I waited.

After a while my neck started to ache from staring up. The rain seemed to come a little harder, but it might have been the wind just blowing it. When I finally saw Shane he appeared shadow-like about twenty feet overhead. He seemed to be standing on one of the small platforms.

"You did it!" I called out.

He didn't answer me. I wiped my face and studied him.

"Shane!" I yelled.

Suddenly he was falling. I heard his body slam the steel deck in a sickening meaty way. Then I saw the dark lump of him mounded beside the derrick. It took me a moment to process what had happened before I was running and kneeling beside him. He lay on his back, and I put my face up close to him and saw that his eyes were open.

"Shane!" I said.

He didn't answer me. I got my arms under his shoulders and dragged him across the rain-slicked steel and into the generator room. I struck a match and held it close. His eyes looked so clean and white against the watery blood running down the side of his mouth. I dropped the match and sat and pulled him into my lap and rested his head on my leg.

"Talk to me," I begged him.

"I did it," he croaked.

I was so relieved to hear him speak that I got choked up.

"I know you did," I said. "You did."

"They'll come for us now."

"Why didn't you wait?" I said. "What was one more day?"

"I was getting worse, Julie. I've been coughing blood. There's something bad wrong with me."

I swallowed and nodded to him.

"But we were so close," I said. "I could have figured out another way."

"It's done now," he said. "All we have to do is wait."

I looked away and wiped the tears from my face.

"I really want to punch you again. Hard."

"Don't. It hurts."

I laughed and sniffled.

Shane coughed and it sounded horrible, like his chest was full of something.

"You're the only person I ever punched," I said. "I've been meaning to tell you that."

"I don't think it'll ever be as good as this again."

"Don't talk like that," I said. "Don't you miss hot food and showers and comfortable beds?"

Shane coughed again.

"I feel really good right now," he said.

"I think you need to stop talking," I said.

He closed his eyes and opened them again. It seemed impossible for him to die now after all we'd accomplished.

"Don't go to sleep," I said. "You can't leave me here alone."

45

THE RAIN STOPPED DURING THE NIGHT AND LEFT THE RIG WET and silent. Shane lay across my lap in the damp darkness of the generator room. I caught myself counting his raspy breaths, expecting each one to be his last. Even without being able to see him, I knew he was seriously hurt and I didn't want to move him.

I didn't sleep. I had no sense of time until dawn slipped over the rig and a faint line of daylight appeared along the base of the door. Shane was still breathing, but I didn't want to wake him. I felt that even speaking to him might tip his fragile condition.

Not long after sunup I checked the time on my watch. It read seven o'clock.

"Julie?" I heard him say.

"Yes."

"Where are we?" he said.

"We're in the generator room."

"Why?"

"Because you fell."

He was quiet for a moment, like he was thinking about it all.

"I broke the light," he said.

"Yeah," I said.

"Are you okay?"

"Yes," I said.

Shane coughed and it sounded horrible. "Nobody came?" he said.

"It was just last night. Please, stop talking."

"You have to go up to the helicopter pad. You have to wait."

I didn't answer.

"Julie?"

"I know," I said.

I couldn't imagine dying alone in such a place. I would have never wanted Shane to leave me if I were in his position.

"Prop the door open for me," he said. "So I can see."

"I'm going to have to get out from under you."

"Okay," he said. "Just go slow."

I eased out from under him and lowered his head to the floor. Then I got up and opened the door, and daylight fell across the room. I propped the door open with a broom handle and turned back to him. The blood was dried around the edges of his mouth, and his chest was rising and falling heavily like it was working against something.

I saw a tarp lying next to the wall and put it under his head for a pillow. I knew it was going to be hard to find my way through the generator room once I left him. And it might be a while before I could return.

"Don't try to move," I said. "I'll be back as soon as I can. I'll bring water."

Shane nodded to me and I turned to go. The truth was, I didn't know how I could return once I used up the matches. But I was fairly certain it wasn't going to matter anyway.

I slowly made my way through the generator room, one match at a time. I knelt and struck each one on the floor, then made about twenty slow, careful steps before it burned to the tip of my glove and I had to drop it. By the time I reached the stairs I had used all but two.

I followed the guide rope to get up to the helipad. Then I sat in the middle of the SOS and pulled my legs up and rested my forehead on my knees. I had no hope that Shane's plan was going to work. The horrible truth was that part of me was relieved not to be with him. I didn't want a person dying in my lap down in that damp, dark steel room. I kept reminding myself that it was Shane who wanted me to leave, but really I'd wanted it, too.

Horror. That was the only word that kept coming to mind.

Shane dying. Being left alone to starve on the rig with the wind whistling through the cold steel and the Gulf swells slurping through the beams below.

It was a horror that paralyzed me.

46

IT WAS AFTER NOON WHEN I HEARD THE THRUMMING OF
propeller blades in the distance. For a while I didn't
look up. When I did, I saw the small black speck of the
helicopter moving toward me. Soon it was hovering
overhead and the force of the rotors threatened to bowl
me over. I saw the pilot studying me curiously and
faintly got the sense he was waiting for me to move. I
didn't, and he finally set the helicopter down at the edge
of the pad. A side door slid open and a man in blue work
pants and a polo shirt ducked out and hurried low in
my direction.

"Who are you?" he yelled.

"Julie Sims," I said.

He shook his head that he couldn't hear me. Then he grabbed my arm and tugged it slightly, as if questioning if I could stand.

I stood and he walked with me down the stairs and started to lead me inside. I pulled away from him before he could get me through the door. When he looked at me I shook my head.

He frowned and leaned close to my ear. "What are you doing here?"

"I floated here," I said.

I heard the rotors starting to slow.

"Are you by yourself?" he asked.

I shook my head. "No," I said. "My friend's with me."

His name was Jim. He was trim and clean-cut like someone in the military. While we waited for the noise of the helicopter to die down he held on to my arm like he was worried I was going to run off. Meanwhile two other rig workers got out of the helicopter and approached us, looking at Jim with puzzled expressions.

"What's going on, Jim?" one of them asked.

I felt weak, like I was about to faint. Jim held up a finger signaling his co-workers to wait a moment.

"Are you okay?" he asked me. "Do you need anything?"

I shook my head.

"Water? Food?"

"No," I said. "I'm fine."

Then the pilot walked up and gathered around me with the other three men.

"Tell us what happened," Jim said to me.

I didn't have the energy to go into it all, so I just gave him the basics. "We were scuba diving out of Gulf Shores, Alabama," I said. "We came up and the boat was gone. We floated out here. There were three of us."

"Where are the others?"

"One drowned. The other one's down below."

"How long have you been here?"

"About a month," I said. "I don't know exactly . . . I had a calendar inside."

Jim motioned with his chin, and the pilot returned to the helicopter and put on his headset. He left the door open and I heard him talking to the Coast Guard, but I couldn't make out what they said. After a moment he took his headset off again and came back to us, nodding to himself in amazement.

"Yep," he said. "They gave up searching for you nearly three weeks ago. They can't believe you made it all the way out here. They're sending a chopper."

"They need to tell my parents I'm alive," I said.

"I'm sure they're doing that right now."

"I want to know that they told them."

The pilot glanced at Jim and Jim nodded to him. "Yeah," the pilot said. "I'll go call them back and get verification."

"My friend's down there," I said. "He's lying inside the generator room."

Jim turned to his co-workers. "Why don't you two go check it out," he said. "I'll stay here with her. Then we'll get her home."

The men, the rig, all of it was getting blurry.

"I'd like to stay until he leaves," I said. "Until they get him."

Jim nodded considerately. "Okay," he said. "I understand."

He studied me closely. Then he put his hand on my shoulder and steadied me. "You sure you're okay?"

47

I HEARD THE DRONE OF THE HELICOPTER AND FELT MYSELF LYING in a cramped space. I opened my eyes and saw Jim and the others sitting forward of me. At first I thought it was a dream, and then I remembered. I sat up, and Jim turned and smiled at me. I noticed they were all wearing headsets. I couldn't speak above the noise, but Jim pointed out the window at a Coast Guard chopper off our left side. Then he opened a bottle of water and handed it to me. He watched me while I drank. Then another man passed a headset back and Jim put it on my head.

"Welcome back," he said.

I took another drink, trying to clear my head.

"We're about ten minutes out," he continued. "We're taking you to the Gulf Shores airport. Your friend's in the Coast Guard chopper. It's continuing on to Brookley Air Force Base, where they'll transfer him to an ambulance."

"Will he be okay?"

"Honestly, I don't know. They've got him stabilized, but he has some internal bleeding."

"They have to save him."

"They're doing all they can," Jim said.

"Do my parents know?"

"They're meeting us on the tarmac."

"Both of them?"

"I assume so. The Coast Guard said *parents*, plural."

It was probably a mistake, I thought. Surely Mom was back in Atlanta. It would be hours before she could make it down. But Dad would be there, his whole goofy self in khaki and plaid.

"Lucky you floated up on that rig," Jim continued.

"Why is it like that?" I said. "The rig, I mean. Why is it empty?"

"They shut it down when the price of oil got too low. Couldn't make money. There's hundreds of abandoned rigs out there. They say maybe they'll start it up again one day, but I doubt it. I think they say that because it's too expensive to take it down."

It made sense, but the idea of such massive waste was hard to understand.

"Good thing for you, huh?" Jim chuckled.

I nodded. Jim looked out the window again. The Coast Guard chopper was starting to peel off to the northwest. Then he turned back to me. "By the way, did you take out that hazard beacon?"

"He did," I said. "My friend did."

"That was pretty smart of him."

"Yeah," I said. "He's smart."

I saw them standing below as we descended to the tarmac. Mom and Dad beside each other, holding hands. I couldn't imagine what she was doing there, but I remembered when they used to stand like that, watching me play in the waves at the beach.

The chopper eased down, and Jim pulled my headset off and helped me up from my place on the floor. Then he opened the door and guided me out, ducking and holding me close against him. In a moment I was in their arms, the three of us squeezed together and crying.

There was a crowd of reporters snapping pictures. They

began asking me questions, but I didn't answer them. Then Dad let go of me and turned to Jim and shook his hand. Jim nodded and pointed to an ambulance parked nearby. Two paramedics were walking toward us.

"Come on, sweetheart," Dad said. "They need to check you out."

The reporters seemed worried that I was going to get away from them before I answered their questions. They came closer and held microphones in my face.

"Leave her alone," Mom demanded with her lawyer voice. "She doesn't feel like talking right now."

To our relief Jim stepped between us. "I'll take your questions over here," he said. "Let them do what they need to do and go home."

The paramedics took me with them to the ambulance and got me to lie on a stretcher inside. They did some tests on me and asked me questions about my health. I took off my gloves and showed them my hands and told them about the cuts on my legs and my scratchy throat from breathing in the mold. They said I needed to go to the hospital to get on antibiotics.

Mom and Dad rode with me, one of them on either side of the stretcher, holding my arms.

"I knew if anybody could make it, you could," Dad said.

"Shane might die, Dad."

"Let's hope not. I talked to his mother, and she's flying in to be with him."

"I should be there, too."

"I think we need to stay out of the doctors' way right now," Dad said.

"We never gave up hope on you," Mom said. "I can't imagine what you've been through."

"Have you been here the whole time?"

Mom looked at Dad like they had something to tell me. "Your father's been sick," she said.

"What's wrong?"

Dad squeezed my hand. "I'm all right now. But that day on the boat, I got sick."

"The anchor pulled," I said. "It was barely clinging. I should have come up."

"It wasn't your fault," he assured me. "After you went down I started having some problems up top. If it wasn't for that, none of this would have happened."

I knew then I was about to finally learn the rest of my story.

"I don't know if you remember, but I was feeling bad," he said. "It was a little more serious than I figured. After I watched you go down, I must have gone back to the wheelhouse. They say they found me in there. But all I remember is waking up in the hospital with some DKA crap."

"Gib," Mom said, frowning. "It's called diabetic keto-acidosis," she continued. "He went into a coma and almost died. Fortunately, a fisherman saw the cabin door swinging open and stopped to check it out."

"The anchor pulled and reset itself," Dad said. "Probably not fifty feet from the tanks."

"But you're okay?"

"Heck, yeah, I'm okay," Dad said. "Now that I got you back."

"He's going to be fine," Mom said. "They've got him on a special diet, and he's watching his insulin more closely. Isn't that right, Gib?"

I detected Mom's motherly tone. It had been a long time since I'd heard any soft feelings in her voice regarding Dad.

"That's right, doll," he said. "Watching it like a hawk."

And I hadn't heard him call Mom that in years. I looked at both of them.

"Mom, are you staying at our house?" I asked.

She didn't answer me. Just then the ambulance pulled into the emergency entrance and stopped. The back doors opened and they began sliding me out.

48

AT THE HOSPITAL THEY PERFORMED TESTS AND DOCTORED MY hands and gave me medicine for mold exposure and malnourishment. It was hours before I was finally taken to a room and left alone. I fell into a deep sleep like my body had died and left my mind trapped in a dark liquid aurora of dreamy snapshots that had no end and no beginning. Until finally I was back at Fort Morgan, surfcasting off the beach. The Gulf waves rolled gently against my toes, and seagulls called and dove into shimmering schools of bait fish.

But the water was strangely empty of boats, and it dawned on me that maybe I was the only person left on earth. I turned back to see Mom and Dad lying on a blanket under the oak tree. At first I was comforted at the sight of them, but then a moment later they were gone. I turned back to look over the water again and saw a dark line of clouds on the horizon, flickering with lightning that made no noise and dragging a long curtain of rain.

I woke to Mom standing over me touching my forehead.

"Julie," she said.

The sight of her and Dad standing behind her washed away the lingering images of the nightmare.

"Are you okay?" Mom asked.

"I'm fine," I said, closing my eyes again.

The next day the doctor told me I was healthy enough to go home. My lungs would probably eventually clear of the mold, and my hands were healing fine. I would have scars, but no tendons were cut and I'd regain full use of them after some therapy.

"What about my friend?" I asked him.

He didn't know anything about Shane. After the staff was finished with me, I joined Mom and Dad in the waiting room, where they were standing with a Coast Guard officer. He was about Dad's age but tall and thin with a mustache.

"Julie," Mom said, "this is Officer Barnett. He'd like to ask you some questions if you feel up to it. Or we can do this later."

"Is Shane okay?" I asked.

"The boy who was with you?"

"Yes."

"Last I heard, he was in stable condition."

"So he'll live?"

"That means the doctors don't really know yet."

I nodded that I understood.

"I'll make this quick," Officer Barnett said. "I know you're ready to get home."

He asked me some questions about the Jordans, and I told him all I knew. Then he expressed his amazement that Shane and I had survived, and I didn't have anything to say to that.

I was thinking, *It just happened like it did. I wasn't in control of any of it. I didn't do anything but stay alive the best I could, like anyone else would have.*

When Officer Barnett was finished he told my parents that he might have some more questions later, but that was all for now. Then he offered us a ride back to the airport, and I finally felt done with all the attention and questions. I desperately wanted to be alone with my parents somewhere familiar. And it wasn't until I was sliding across the seat into Brownie, breathing in its wet-towel smell and squeezing in next to Dad as Mom climbed in beside me, that I felt like I was truly home.

"Do you want to stop and get anything?" Mom asked.

"No," I said. "I just want to go home."

Dad patted my hair and put his arm around me. "Me too, sweetheart," he said.

Dad helped me to my old bedroom, with Mom following. The air conditioner in the window had the room cool and pleasantly full of comforting background noise. I climbed under the sheets and buried my head into the pillow. Then Dad pulled the quilt up to my shoulders and patted me on the back.

"We'll be here when you wake up," he said.

Dad left the room, and Mom came to sit on the bed beside me.

"What's going on?" I asked her.

"What do you mean?"

"What happened with you and Dad while I was gone?"

She kept her hand on me but looked away at the window. "He's got to take care of himself, Julie," she said.

"I'm not worrying about it all anymore, Mom. There's nothing I can do."

"He says he's going to take his health more seriously."

"It was never about the tanks, was it?"

She shook her head. "No," she said. "It was about me. I think I was jealous."

"What do you mean?"

She thought about it for a moment. "You know, Julie," she said, "there's two kinds of people in this world. There are those who make things happen and those who watch things happen. Your dad's a doer. And it's taken me a while to admit that I'm just a watcher."

"But you're a good lawyer. You made that happen."

"That's no dream. It's only a job. A crappy one."

"Did you quit?"

"Your dad needs me. I need his dreams. Life isn't life without them. And if he can give me the dreams, I think I can hold the rest together."

I sat up and hugged her. She squeezed me tight and I sobbed against her shoulder.

"I want it to be like it was," I said once the tears had stopped.

"Me too," she said.

"I don't want to go back to Atlanta," I said.

I heard Mom sniffle and breathe deep through her nose. "We're going to try again," she said.

"No, you're going to make it work this time. Both of you. That's his biggest dream of all. He'll do anything you say."

"I know, sweetheart," she said. "I know. And I'm here."

49

I STAYED AT THE HOUSE AND RESTED AND RECOVERED. I desperately wanted to know how Shane was doing. I tried calling the hospital about him but I was told they couldn't release any information. I had Mom call Officer Barnett and he said he knew Shane was in stable condition but that he couldn't find out anything more. Then I looked up his home phone number in my old elementary school directory, but when I called I got a recording saying it was disconnected. Finally, on the morning of the third day, Dad came into my room and held out his cell phone to me.

"It's Mrs. Jordan," he said. "She wants to talk to you."

I studied him curiously as I took the phone.

"Julie?" a woman's voice said to me. "This is Carol Jordan, Shane's mom."

"Hi," I said.

"I know you've been calling the hospital. I wanted to tell you personally that Shane is recovering. And I want to thank you for all you did."

"So he's going to be okay?"

"Yes," she said. "He's got some broken ribs and a concussion, but they've stopped the internal bleeding."

"Can I come visit him?"

"Yes," she said. "He'd like that very much. And I'd love to meet you."

Dad drove me to the hospital that afternoon, where we met Mrs. Jordan in the waiting room. She was very pretty and much younger-looking than I expected. We followed her down the hallway to a large room, where we found Shane lying in bed with IVs in his arm and bandages up to his neck. He smiled at me.

"How you doing, kid?" Dad said with good humor.

"Fine, Mr. Sims."

"That's good to hear. Thank you for taking care of my girl out there."

"I'd have died if it weren't for her."

"Well, sounds like you make a good team."

"Yes, sir," he said.

"All right, then. Get to feeling better again. You two catch up while Mrs. Jordan and I meet with Officer Barnett in the cafeteria and sign off on a few things."

Dad and Mrs. Jordan walked out and left us alone. At first it was awkward. I didn't know where to begin.

"Your mom's nice," I said.

"Yeah," he said. "She's pretty messed up about what happened to Dad."

"I didn't see her boyfriend," I said.

"You didn't?"

"No. Is there one, really?"

"I haven't asked her yet. You think I should?"

I smiled and shook my head. "No. Not yet."

"I told you breaking that stupid light would work."

"You got lucky."

We laughed. It was a relief that we were both still the same even after being swept into real life again.

"So when are you leaving?" I asked.

"I guess when I can walk again," Shane joked.

"I mean, smart-aleck, when are you leaving for school?"

"August twenty-third."

"You going to cut your hair?"

"Maybe. You want me to?"

"Just a little bit. Not much."

"I thought you were going to do it," he said.

"When do you come home from boarding school?"

"It's just Bay St. Louis, a couple of hours away. I can come home on the weekends."

"So when you come home, I'll cut it."

"But you'll be in Atlanta."

"No," I said. "I'm staying here."

"Really?"

I smiled and nodded. "Yeah. With Mom and Dad."

He studied me for a second. After all our talks out on the rig, I knew I didn't have to explain anything to him.

"It all worked out, didn't it?" he said.

"I think so," I said.

"Now I just have to fit in at a new school."

"You'll do it," I said.

"I'll do my best."

I realized right then that all Shane had ever done was his best. And now I was sure his best was only going to get better.

50

ON THE RIDE HOME DAD DROVE THE BEACH ROAD. THE SKY WAS clear, and through my open window I saw the Gulf waves rolling gently over the sand. Tourist cars lined the way, and I could hear the scattered voices of children and see several kites flutter over the dunes.

Dad pulled into the dive shop. I hadn't seen it since the morning of our accident. He turned off Brownie and sat there for a moment, staring at the sign on the front door: CLOSED UNTIL FURTHER NOTICE.

"Dad?" I finally said.

"I'm not sure what to do about it anymore, Julie."

"What do you mean?"

"I mean, here we are. We've got the Malzon tanks. Your mother's back. And now I wonder if it's all worthwhile."

"Have you paid the bills?"

"Your mother came over and went through everything. She said she got most of it handled."

"How's the *Barbie Doll*?"

"Well, with everything that's been going on—you know, with you missing and my health being bad—I haven't taken any trips out since the accident."

"You want to check on it?"

"Sort of," he said. "Sort of not."

"Come on," I said. "We can't just let her rot and sink out there."

I got out of the pickup and heard Dad get out behind me. He followed me around the side of the building, where I stopped and gazed out at the bayou while waiting for him to catch up. The *Barbie Doll* floated safely in her usual spot, though I could already tell from a distance that she was starting to gather mildew on her white paint and gray oxidation splotches on her hardware.

"We ought to at least crank it up, I guess," Dad said, "while we're here."

I continued toward the dock and sensed Dad dragging behind like a part of him was reluctant to approach. I stepped down onto the stern deck and felt the old boat sway and creak like it had gotten a lot older in just the time I'd been gone.

I turned back to see Dad standing above me on the dock. "You coming?"

He didn't answer me, and I saw he was tearing up.

"What's wrong?" I asked.

He wiped his eyes with the back of his hand and I could tell he was struggling to keep from crying in front of me.

"I just didn't know," he said, wiping his eyes again. "I just didn't know how it would be when you got back."

"I don't understand," I said.

"I mean, we don't have to do this. It's not important to me anymore. Not if you don't want to. I wouldn't mind if you never wanted to go out on the water again."

"It wasn't your fault, Dad. I don't feel that way."

"You don't?"

I shook my head. "I just know what you always taught me was right. You have to be safe out there. And even that's not always enough. But it's no reason to quit doing what you love."

"So you'd go out there again?"

"I was scared. I was scared the whole time. But never once did I want either one of us to give up what we do. Yes, of course I'll go out there again."

Dad nodded to himself and sniffled. He stepped down onto the deck and looked around at the boat like it was something he was thinking about buying. A boat he was seeing for the first time.

"You really feel that way?" he said.

"Yes," I said. "And so does Mom. She came back for us to do this. To try to make it work. To make it all *really* work."

Dad didn't look at me, but he reached over and put his big arm around me and pulled me close. Then I felt myself starting to tear up, too. I felt how much he wanted us all together again and how empty and worthless his life had been without Mom and me. Now I knew why I had fought so hard to survive both in the water and on the rig. I had two people back on land who needed me to come home.

He gave me a final squeeze and backed away. "All right," he said. "Let's get started."

THE INSPIRATION BEHIND *DEEP WATER*

WHEN I WAS SIXTEEN YEARS OLD I WAS STRANDED AFTER A scuba dive, a situation resulting from circumstances much like you find in this story.

Two friends and I had taken a seventeen-foot boat nine miles out into the Gulf of Mexico. We didn't have a GPS or any navigation electronics on board. All we had was a compass. We had been told by a scuba instructor that if we headed due south from Orange Beach, Alabama, until we could no longer see land we would be nine miles offshore and in proximity of a sunken ship called the *Allen*. The *Allen* is 440 feet long, one of several World War II supply ships sunk in 90 feet of water to create an artificial reef for recreational purposes. These ships are popular with fishermen and scuba divers. Our plan was to get out there early and find a commercial dive charter already anchored. Then, once they finished their dives, we'd hurry over and take their place.

My friend Archie and I had been certified scuba divers for a couple of years. Also with us was a boy from Mississippi named Dean, whom I'd just met. Dean was the son of one of my mother's school friends, in town for a brief visit. He didn't know much about boats, much less scuba diving. He just happened to be along for the ride.

That day the Gulf was a calm surface of gentle swells and the skies were blue. Once we lost sight of land it didn't take long to locate a charter boat flying the red-and-white dive flag that means they're anchored with divers in the water. We kept our distance until we saw them preparing to leave. Then we pulled alongside and dropped our own anchor just as they were pulling away.

The water was clear enough to see the anchor rope streaming down toward the seafloor, but not so clear that we could see the ship below. It took about thirty seconds for all the rope to spool out. Then Archie put the boat in reverse to make sure the anchor was set and holding. We saw right away that it wasn't. And just a pull on the rope revealed that it hadn't even touched bottom.

Fortunately the current wasn't bad, so we had time to

lengthen the anchor rope with a ski rope and drop it again before we drifted too far out of position. Then Archie and I got into our scuba gear, grabbed our spearguns, and rolled off. We swam down the anchor rope and soon found ourselves facing the giant sunken hull of the *Allen*.

We had a great dive. The visibility was good and we speared a stringerful of fish. But when we returned to the anchor to start our ascent, we knew right away that something was wrong. The anchor rope, our lifeline to the surface, was limp. It had either broken or come untied.

We couldn't afford to analyze what happened. We were running out of air and about to exceed the safe time limit for ninety feet. We had no choice but to start a free ascent immediately. Scuba ascents are done slowly so that your body has time to release deadly gases that have built up in your system during the dive. It was going to take us nearly twenty minutes to reach the surface. With free ascents it's hard to control how fast you're rising, and all the while the current is sweeping you away from the dive site. By the time we surfaced we were going to be tired and maybe lost.

When we finally broke into sunlight there was no one to be seen. The current wasn't bad, so we doubted that we'd drifted far, but who knew how long it would take Dean to realize something was wrong. And even when he did realize it, we didn't know if he could drive a boat.

The first thing we did was get rid of our fish so that the blood wouldn't attract predators. Then I hung my mask at the end of my speargun and began waving it in the air while Archie watched below us for sharks.

After about fifteen minutes, in an unbelievable stroke of luck, a fishing boat happened to pass by and see us. We told the fishermen what happened, and from the higher vantage point of their boat, they were able to see Dean drifting about a quarter-mile away. They got us out of the water and took us to our boat, ending what could have been the start of our own *Deep Water* adventure.

As we suspected, Dean had never even known anything was wrong. After pulling up the ski rope, we saw that it and the anchor rope had come untied.

I've often wondered what would have happened that day if the fishing boat hadn't come along—if we hadn't been so fortunate. And that's where this story came from.

GOFISH

Watt Key

What did you want to be when you grew up?
I wanted to be a writer from a young age and don't recall ever wanting to be anything else.

When did you realize you wanted to be a writer?
I started writing short stories when I was about ten years old. I continued to do this until I was a senior in high school, and my English teacher praised my work and told me she thought that I should become a writer. This was the first time anyone suggested that I was exceptional at anything. With this encouragement I began to write novels and set my sights on getting published and seeing a book I wrote in the library. The image of my book on a library shelf was my idea of success.

What were your hobbies as a kid? What are your hobbies now?
I have always loved the outdoors—hunting and fishing and camping. When I was a kid, in addition to writing stories, I enjoyed drawing and painting. I hope to get back to that someday and make my own illustrations.

Did you play sports as a kid?

I've always been into solo sports for some reason. My favorites as a kid were water skiing and tennis. I was best at cross country, but I never enjoyed it. I haven't water skied in years, but I still play tennis often.

What was your first job, and what was your "worst" job?

My brothers and sisters and I always had chores assigned to us that we didn't get paid for. My first duties were emptying the wastebaskets around the house, feeding various pets (we had lots of animals), and raking and mowing the lawn. I landed my first paying job when I was about eight years old. I was the fly killer for the snack bar at the resort not far from my home. I killed them with a washcloth, stored them in a paper cup, and received ten cents per fly. As soon as I would get enough dimes, I would cash in my pay for a drink to quench my thirst.

My worst job was a stint at the shipyards in Mobile, Alabama, when I was eighteen years old. It was the only summer job I could find when I returned from my freshman year in college. On most days it was over a hundred degrees outside, yet I had to wear steel-toe boots, long pants, a long-sleeve shirt, leather gloves, a hard hat, and safety glasses. This was to protect one from getting burned by the welding sparks that flew about among many other dangers. The ships, most of them hundreds of feet long, were in dry dock supported on giant pillars. My responsibility was to push a wheelbarrow beneath the ships and haul away scrap metal discarded by the welders. It was the hottest, heaviest, most headache-inducing, bone-tiring work I'd ever done in my life. I was often so sweat-drenched and delirious that I could barely focus. I had only been at this assignment a few days before I was surprised by a five-hundred-pound, red-hot slab of sheet metal falling from above and landing not ten feet from me. That's the only job I've ever quit in my life. I truly thought I was going to be killed. And that experience reinforced my commitment to finish college so that I would have more employment choices in the future.

What book is on your nightstand now?
A Land Remembered by Patrick D. Smith

How did you celebrate publishing your first book?
My wife and I went to the Mexican restaurant up the street. It was a fairly low-key celebration. It took a while for me to accept that I'd gotten a legitimate book deal. You may have seen the episode of *The Waltons* when John-Boy gets scammed by the vanity publisher. He told all of his friends and family that he'd gotten a book deal, and they had a big celebration for him. Then he got a letter from the publisher asking him how many of his books he wanted to pay them to print. It was a scam. This exact thing happened to me years before I sold *Alabama Moon*, and it was very embarrassing and eye-opening.

Where do you write your books?
I have a utility shed in my backyard that I finished out as an office. It has electricity and air-conditioning and sometimes internet (I get it wirelessly from the house and the signal is weak at best). I'm most productive when the internet isn't working and I'm not tempted to Google around.

What is your favorite word?
Gloam

Who is your favorite fictional character?
Tarzan

**What was your favorite book when you were a kid?
Do you have a favorite book now?**
Where the Red Fern Grows by Wilson Rawls. That was the book that really did it for me. Ever since then I've wanted to make books like that. It made me want to be a writer.

What's the best advice you have ever received about writing?
Continue to write even when you don't feel like it. If you're a real writer, that's what you have to do. I knew this on an instinctive level for many years, but never heard it described as well as what a painter friend of mine told me. I was watching him create an oil painting of an outdoor scene. He was doing his work in a small, rocking boat, crouched beneath an umbrella in the pouring rain. I remarked that he was the most dedicated artist I'd ever met. He responded by telling me that he wasn't an artist, he was a professional painter.

What advice do you wish someone had given you when you were younger?
I think my parents told me most of these, but so far these are my top ten pieces of advice for my own kids:

1. Top three (legal) things not to do:
   a. Tobacco
   b. Drugs
   c. Lie
2. Always return things better than you found them.
3. Write thank-you notes.

4. Don't lie in bed thinking about a problem. Get up and do something about it. At least get up. And:
   a. Make a list of your problem and three solutions.
   b. You'll probably discover it's not as insurmountable as you thought.
   c. Go back to sleep.
5. It's better not to have an opinion on something you know little about. Proper response—"I'm not sure about that. I haven't studied the issue."
6. Have goals.
7. Do what you say you are going to do.
8. Productivity is 80% time management.
9. Remember that crazy people don't know they're crazy.
10. Always be punctual. Your time is no more valuable than the other person's—no matter who they are.

Do you ever get writer's block? What do you do to get back on track?

To me "writer's block" is a condition when a writer who used to write can no longer write. I get stuck on certain stories, but I've never thought of it as writer's block. If I find myself stuck, it's usually because I haven't developed my characters well enough and I'm bored with the story. And if I'm bored with it, my readers are going to be bored with it. I either start over or work on something else. Several times I've found myself stuck halfway through a project, moved on to something else, and never returned. I have a messy trail of paper I've left over the years that will never be finished or published, and I can only look back at it as practice.

What do you want readers to remember about your books?

That my books made them want to read more books.

What would you do if you ever stopped writing?
Read and fish more.

If you were a superhero, what would your superpower be?
I don't think this power would make for a good superhero, but I wish I didn't have to sleep or eat. I could get so much more done.

Do you have any strange or funny habits? Did you when you were a kid?
I'm left handed, so I've always found it easier to write in spiral bound notebooks from back to front, using the back of the page. Otherwise my hand rests uncomfortably on the wire binding. My teachers were often confused when I turned in my assignments and they opened my notebook to find it seemingly empty.

When I am revising my books, I print them out many times to handwrite changes and visualize the story arc and layout. I punch holes on the right side of the pages and put the manuscript in a three-ring binder, backwards. And like the spiral notebooks, I read and write from back to front.

What would your readers be most surprised to learn about you?
I like to write computer programs as much as I like writing books. I was a computer science major in college.

The government is the enemy. Or so Moon's father said before his death out in the wilderness. Now Moon must follow his father's last request to seek others like them in Alaska.

But once he's alone, Moon becomes the property of the government he had avoided all his life, caught in a world he does not understand.

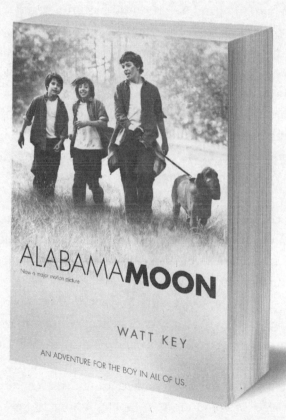

ALABAMA**MOON**

Now a major motion picture

WATT KEY

AN ADVENTURE FOR THE BOY IN ALL OF US.

Keep reading for an excerpt.

It seemed like everything started going wrong the summer before Pap's accident. We heard through Mr. Abroscotto, who owned the general store in Gainesville, that International Paper Company had run into hard times and was selling off some of its land. Pap said that the paper company had owned the forest as long as we'd been there and that they were too big to know about us. If they sold out to smaller landowners, we'd likely be found.

I could tell that Pap was worried. He told me that the swimming hole was off limits and that I was to stay close to the shelter unless I was checking traps or getting drinking water. Without the creek to swim in, the days were hotter than any I can remember. We spent afternoons sitting in the shelter, covered with the tannic acid from boiled acorns to keep off the ticks and mosquitoes. Pap had me practice my reading while he carved fish hooks from briars and bound sticks to make catfish traps.

It wasn't two weeks after our visit to Mr. Abroscotto's store that surveyors found our shelter while we were out checking the traps. When Pap and I returned, we saw their orange vests through the trees and we ducked into the bushes and watched them as they walked around the shelter. They stayed there for about an hour, poking at our things. I asked Pap if they were the government, and he said no, but they weren't much better.

"Should we shoot at 'em?"

"No."

"If they're not any better than—"

"When the war comes, you'll know."

"How?"

"I'll tell you."

The next morning, Pap woke me at daybreak. "Get up," he said. "We need to go into town and find out what's happenin'."

I got excited about going to Mr. Abroscotto's. It was the only time I saw any of the outside world. But I was careful not to let Pap know how I felt. He said showing ourselves to outsiders was the most dangerous part of how we lived. One slipup and the law would be all over us. A trip to the store wasn't anything he wanted to see me excited over.

"We gonna take somethin' to sell, Pap?"

"Ain't got time. Get your britches on."

As the sun slipped over the trees, we made the six-mile trip to Mr. Abroscotto's. We used to sell our furs to him, but it had been more than three years since we'd sold any. He said the prices were so low that he lost money just paying for gasoline to get them to Birmingham, where he sold them to companies that made clothes and things out of them. Since then, we had sold him the meat instead, along with vegetables we grew in the garden, and we bought what we wanted of the outside world with the money he gave us.

Most of the journey was through the forest, but the last half mile was on the road to avoid the big swamp. Pap said this was okay because the road was straight and long and we could hear cars coming in either direction before they saw us. We had time to slip down into the ditch and lie still until they passed.

The store was on the outskirts of town, and the only building nearby was a small brick one that Pap said was owned by the power company. We could see a traffic light another half mile up the road which Pap said was the only one in Gainesville. I liked to watch the light as long as I could before Pap hurried me past the gas pumps and into the store. I'd seen a tractor go under the light once and even a yellow school bus.

Mr. Abroscotto was a strong man for somebody his age, like he used to be a logger or a policeman. His skin was dark as leather and his snow-white hair stood out against it. This time he told us that a lawyer named Mr. Wellington had purchased eleven thousand acres from the paper company. The property went from the Noxubee River to the big swamp and from the highway to Major's Creek on the east and west sides. By Mr. Abroscotto's landmarks, I figured our shelter was just about in the middle of Mr. Wellington's property. Pap must have been thinking the same thing. He walked out of the store without even saying goodbye. I hurried after him and had to walk fast to keep up.

"Slow down, Pap."

He didn't answer me.

"Pap?"

He turned quickly and grabbed my arm and jerked me along beside him. "You keep up this time," he said. "Run if you have to."

———

A couple of weeks passed before heavy equipment started making a road and a clearing three miles away. Pap was nervous all the time and snapped at me when I made the smallest mistake. He got particular about me stepping on sticks and making noise when we walked through the forest. He kept stopping and touching my shoulder, which meant for me to be still and listen. I could tell by the way he acted that all those workers and equipment meant trouble.

We began to check our catfish traps at night, slipping down the banks of the Noxubee River by moonlight. In the mornings we remained close to the shelter unless we had something special to do. We worked the garden, tending our cucumbers, eggplant, and beets. All of those vegetables, when spaced the right way, grew hidden among the natural forest plants and wouldn't give us away if someone was to come across them. In the heat of the day, we'd get back into the shelter again and stay there until late afternoon. Pap began to watch and listen out the window slits as much as he worked on things. Even my reading began to make him nervous.

"Read to yourself, boy. You're too old to read out loud anymore."

A month later, Pap and I were traveling a trail to the southeast of the shelter to get some red clay for pot making. We were less than a mile from the new clearing when Pap suddenly held his hand up in the air. I knew the signal and stopped. We stood there for several seconds and then, through the whine of mosquitoes, I heard hammering.

"Somebody's makin' somethin', Pap?"

I saw him clench his teeth and narrow his eyes. "Shhh!" he said.

After a few more seconds, Pap continued down the trail.

"What is it, Pap?"

"House."

"Somebody gonna live there?"

"Yeah."

I could tell Pap didn't want to talk about it, so I followed behind him and didn't ask any more questions.

After we heard the hammering, Pap couldn't keep his mind on his chores. He'd get me to working on something at the shelter and he'd say he had to walk off in the woods and tend to things. He was usually gone for a couple of hours. He didn't want me to know where he went, but I knew it was to watch the hammering.

One day he said, "You finish scalin' those fish. I got to go look for somethin' I left down the trail."

"I wanna go, Pap."

"Just a one-man job."

"I've only got two fish left."

Pap stared off at the treetops and bit his bottom lip. "All right," he finally said. "Come on, then."

Pap never meant to look for anything. We slipped through the forest using gallberry and cane for cover until we got to where the house was being built. They had cemented concrete blocks together and run timbers across them for the floor supports. The yard was stacked with lumber for the rest of the framing. I turned to Pap, waiting for him to tell me what it meant. His face was worried pale.

"Gonna be a big house, Pap?" I finally asked.

"Big huntin' lodge," he mumbled.

"I've never seen somethin' built that big."

He nodded his head and motioned for us to head back to the shelter.

We didn't go to the lodge together again. The days began to grow cooler and the breezes told us that fall was arriving. Things had changed between Pap and me. Even though I was with him just about every minute of the day, I didn't feel like he knew I was there. He was far away in thought most of the time, and even though I watched his face, I couldn't get clues to what he was thinking.

We got the steel traps out of storage and oiled them and wired the parts that were broken. The maple leaves had just started to turn and I knew we were over a month away from trapping season. But Pap didn't seem to be doing things in the right order anymore. One day he told me to go gather mulberries. It had been five months since the last mulberry dropped.

"Pap, there's not any mulberries."

"Just do what I tell you," he said.

I waited for a few seconds to see if he would realize his mistake, but he went back to sharpening his knife. I didn't know what to do, so I stepped into the forest and started walking, thinking that if I stayed gone long enough it would convince him that I'd tried my best.

Once I got away from the shelter, it felt good to be on my own again after such a long time staying close to Pap and feeling his worries. I looked up into the trees and studied the yellows and reds of the changing leaves. The birds flitted about and made shrill cries from deep in the bush. It felt like I could breathe easier, and the smells of cedar and stinkbugs flowed into my nose.

Without meaning to, I wandered within hearing distance of the lodge. Once the sound of power tools and hammers reached my ears, I was too curious not to slip closer for a better look.

The workmen had moved a house trailer onto the site, and they seemed to be living in it. More lumber was stacked in the yard, along with roofing material and bricks. The lodge was already framed two stories high. I wanted to stay and watch the men working, but Pap's warnings about contact with outsiders started to play in my head. I crept back into the forest and took a different trail to the shelter.

Pap was sitting outside, weaving a basket from muscadine vine when I walked up. I stood in front of him, ready to tell him why I didn't have any mulberries, but he didn't ask about them or anything else.

Finally I said, "They're puttin' walls on that lodge, Pap."

His fingers stopped and he looked up at me. "I don't ever want you goin' near it again."

"But it's not even finished."

"I don't care. You heard what I said."

"You think maybe when the lawyer moves in we could talk to him and he'd let us stay on?"

Pap looked at me again. "I don't know, son! Why don't you get back to work and forget about that lawyer and his business."

———

As fall passed, the leaves began dropping from the trees and the forest canopy became a solid green fan of pine needles. We pulled our deerskin jackets from between the cedar boards and waterproofed them with mink oil for the season. The carrots would stay in the ground for a while longer, but the other garden vegetables needed to come out before the first frost. I was always excited about the last harvest of the year because I knew it meant we'd go to Mr. Abroscotto's store to sell whatever we had.

I was afraid that Pap might tell me to stay behind, but he didn't. He shouldered the sack of vegetables one morning and told me to get my jacket and come with him. Pap would usually be walking slow and studying the forest. He'd look for deer scrapes and hog rootings and any other signs that might help us find game once the weather turned cold. But that day his mind was on other things and he stared straight ahead and didn't slow down.

Mr. Abroscotto was sitting behind the counter reading a newspaper when we walked in.

"Mornin', George," Pap said.

Mr. Abroscotto set down his paper and stood up. "Mornin', Oli. How you, Moon?"

"I'm fine," I said.

"What do you two have for me?"

Pap showed Mr. Abroscotto the sack of vegetables. "Cucumbers, eggplant, and beets," he said.

Mr. Abroscotto took the sack to the scales. He weighed the vegetables separately and then put them all in a brown box on the floor.

"How does twenty bucks sound?" he said.

"If that's what you can do, I don't guess we've got much choice."

Mr. Abroscotto nodded and paid him from the register. Pap fidgeted the money into his pocket, and I knew he was in a better mood.

"What more have you heard about that lawyer?" Pap asked.

Mr. Abroscotto shook his head. "Haven't heard much. See his workmen in here all the time."

"You know when they're gonna be done?"

"They're tellin' me December. Gonna be moved in for Christmas."

I stood behind Pap and looked around the store at the shelves of candy and canned food. I was careful not to let Pap see me, because I knew it would make him snap at me. Sometimes he made me wait outside while he went in and traded. He said it was too tempting for a boy inside the store.

"What's he gonna do with that big place?" Pap asked.

"I hear he likes to squirrel hunt."

Pap shook his head and looked mad. "All that to hunt squirrels?"

"Guess some people got more money than they know what to do with."

"Guess so," Pap grumbled. "Let me have some salt, some .22 bullets, vinegar, box of nails, and matches."

Mr. Abroscotto left to collect our supplies.

"How about some sugar this time, Pap?"

"Don't need sugar."

"How about some canned peas like we had that one time?"

"We've got a pile of toasted acorns you haven't touched yet."

I figured he wasn't in the mood to buy extras. "We've got everything we need already, don't we, Pap?"

Pap nodded. "Got everything we need," he repeated.

We walked back up the road and into the forest, where we took a trail that I liked through a grove of cedars and tall field grass. That was the last time Pap left the forest.

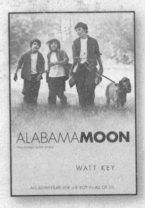

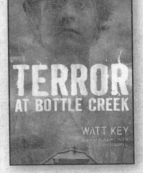